FULL
THRUTTLE

Hover Car Racer

Also by Matthew Reilly

Ice Station
Temple
Contest
Area 7
Scarecrow

Hover Car Racer: *Crash Course*

FULL THRUTTLE

Hover Car Racer

BY MATTHEW REILLY

Illustrated by Pablo Raimondi

Aladdin Paperbacks

New York London Toronto Sydney

For Matt Martin

ALADDIN PAPERBACKS
An imprint of Simon & Schuster Children's Publishing Division
1230 Avenue of the Americas, New York, NY 10020
Text copyright © 2004 by Karanadon Entertainment Pty Ltd.
Illustrations copyright © 2006 by Pablo Raimondi
Text previously published in Australia in 2004
by Pan Macmillan Australia Pty Limited
All rights reserved, including the right of reproduction in whole or
in part in any form.
ALADDIN PAPERBACKS and colophon are trademarks of
Simon & Schuster, Inc.
The text of this book was set in Sabon.
Manufactured in the United States of America
First Aladdin Paperbacks edition October 2006
2 4 6 8 10 9 7 5 3 1
Library of Congress Control Number 2006923717
ISBN-13: 978-1-4169-0228-7
ISBN-10: 1-4169-0228-7

Jason Chaser has the need for speed—hyper speed. And with his little brother, the Bug, navigating, the fourteen-year-old hover car racing phenom—in his car, the *Argonaut*—is geared up to take the world by storm. Jason's first stop, however, is the prestigious International Race School, which he is invited to attend after impressing one of it's instructors, ex-pro-racer Scott Syracuse, with his considerable driving talents during one of the schools qualifying events. But getting into the school is just the beginning. Once there, Jason and the Bug are teamed up with mech chief Sally McDuff, and Jason soon finds himself matching his skill against some of the planet's best amateur, teenage fliers. Included in that mix are Jason's hometown rival and all-around cretin, Barnaby Becker; American pilot Ariel Piper, the first girl ever to be accepted into Race School; and the mysterious driver in black, prince Xavier Xonora, who never seems to lose and who has partnered up with Becker. And as if the competition with his classmates isn't enough, Jason also has to contend with demanding instructors, of which Scott Syracuse turns out to be the most difficult, and sabotaged equipment courtesy of the equipment department. Despite these challenges, Jason manages to qualify—barely—for the School's annual Sponsors' race.

FOR A COMPLETE DESCRIPTION OF THE EVENTS
LEADING UP TO THE START OF THIS BOOK READ
HOVER CAR RACER: *CRASH COURSE.*

PART I

THE TOURNAMENT

The Bug squealed with delight.

CHOOKA'S CHARCOAL CHICKEN RESTAURANT
HOBART, TASMANIA

The Bug squealed with delight as he popped the top off his well-shaken can of Coke and sprayed it into the air like a triumphant pro racer on the winner's podium uncorking a bottle of Moët champagne.

Beside him, Jason and Henry Chaser cheered; threw their fists into the air.

It was Thursday night and the Chaser family was celebrating Team *Argonaut*'s win in Race 25, and its subsequent qualification for the Sponsors' Tournament on the coming Saturday.

Family tradition dictated that it was "winner's choice"— the family member (or members) being celebrated got to choose the restaurant and the Bug had quickly chosen his favorite restaurant in all the world: the chicken burger chain, Chooka's Charcoal Chicken.

Which was why the entire family—plus Sally McDuff, who was by now an honorary Chaser anyway—now sat around a plain formica table surrounded by the remains of chicken burger wrappers, onion rings, french fries, and Coke cans. Everyone was laughing and smiling and recounting their favorite moments of the nail-biting race.

Well, not quite.

At one stage in the dinner, Jason noticed that his mother wasn't joining in the festivities but was, rather, staring off into space, seemingly lost in thought.

"Are you all right, Mom?" he asked.

She turned abruptly, as if roused from a dream, and quickly regathered her smile. "I'm fine, dear. Just thrilled for you boys."

The world had been spinning for Jason since his down-to-the-wire, skip-the-last-pit-stop win over Prince Xavier earlier that day. His memories of the afternoon were a blur of images:

He remembered returning to the pits after the race, being lifted out of the *Argonaut* by a jubilant Sally, high-fiving the Bug, standing on the podium in his battered boots and denim overalls, and watching on the big screen as the 10 points Team *Argonaut* received for winning elevated the *Argonaut* to 12th in the Championship Standings.

He also recalled Scott Syracuse coming over to him after the victor's presentation, and looking at him closely.

"You skipped your last pit stop again, Mr. Chaser."

"Yes, sir. I did."

"You weren't worried about making the same mistake twice?"

"No, sir. I knew I could make it this time."

"So you decided not to take my counsel?"

"No, sir. I just decided to follow something else you told me about mistakes, way back when we were doing pit practice and I kept creeping out of my pit bay."

Syracuse frowned. "What was my advice then?"

"You said I shouldn't resist my mistakes. That I should learn from them. So I decided to learn from my last mistake—the other time I skipped my last pit stop, I shouldn't have. This time, it was okay."

"By exactly 1.64 inches . . ." Syracuse observed.

Jason smiled. "My dad once told me you can win by an inch or a mile, sir. Either way, it's still a win."

And with that, for the first time Jason could remember, Scott Syracuse smiled.

He nodded graciously. "Well done today, Mr. Chaser. I can't possibly imagine what awaits us when you race in Saturday's tournament."

He began to walk away.

"Mr. Syracuse!" Jason called after him. "My family's in town and we're going out to celebrate tonight." He paused. "Wanna come?"

Syracuse hesitated for a moment, as if this were the most unexpected question in the world for him.

"Sure," he said at last. "That'd be . . . very nice. What time?"

Jason told him.

Syracuse said, "Well, I have some work to do, some lessons to prepare, so I might be a little late. But I'll be there."

And sure enough, Syracuse arrived at the restaurant exactly forty-five minutes late, just as a classic Chooka's ice-cream cake with the *Argonaut*'s number 55 on it was delivered to their table.

As Syracuse joined them, Jason wondered if he ate takeout chicken burgers very often. As it turned out, Syracuse handled his greasy burger with ease.

It took all of four seconds for Henry Chaser, official armchair racing expert, to start asking Syracuse all about his professional career.

"You know," Henry said, "we were talking about that time you tried to cut the heel in Italy once. That time you got caught in there for—what was it—four hours?"

"Four and a half," Syracuse corrected.

"What happened?"

Jason also waited for the answer.

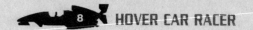

When he spoke, Syracuse seemed to choose his words carefully: "Let's just say, I didn't expect my career to end in New York later that year."

And with that he looked to Jason, as if expecting him to deduce what such a cryptic answer meant.

Jason thought about it.

"You didn't expect to crash out later that year in New York," he repeated aloud. "Which means you expected to race in Italy again, in future years . . ."

"Correct."

Then it hit Jason.

"No *way* . . ."

Syracuse nodded slowly. "You've got it."

"You were doing *research*," Jason said. "You were *reconnoitering* the Italian shortcut for the next year."

Syracuse nodded, impressed. "Well done, Mr. Chaser. To this day, you're the first person to have figured that out."

Jason couldn't believe it. It was so deviously clever. He said: "Everyone thought your taking the shortcut was a desperate attempt to catch the leaders, but it wasn't. You had no intention of catching the leaders at all, or even winning the race. You spent four hours searching the maze, working out its secrets *so you could use them in future years.*"

"Four and a half hours, thank you very much," Syracuse said. "And then Alessandro Romba wiped me out in New York later that season and I never got to use that knowledge. Tough break. But I thought your use of the shortcut in today's race—following that Xavier fellow in—was just as clever. I hope you were taking notes as you went through. Because that knowledge will be with you whenever that shortcut is used from now on—well, at least until the school reconfigures it."

Jason beamed at Syracuse's praise, and glanced over at his father, recalling his words from two days earlier: "When you start learning as hard as you can, I guarantee he'll start treating you differently."

Henry Chaser knew how much it meant. He just smiled knowingly.

Beside Henry, however, Martha Chaser had become lost in her thoughts again.

• • •

At length, Scott Syracuse stood up from the table. "Thank you all for a lovely dinner, but I fear I have to go."

"Hey, thanks for coming," Jason said.

"Don't stay out too late, Mr. Chaser. Just because you qualified for the big tournament on Saturday doesn't get you out of classes tomorrow. Lessons will take place as usual."

"Aw! Don't you ever take a break?" Jason asked.

"See you in the morning, Mr. Chaser. Good night, everyone."

THE INTERNATIONAL RACE SCHOOL
HOBART, TASMANIA
FRIDAY, MAY 31

The next day was like an episode of that old TV show, *Lifestyles of the Rich and Famous*—albeit an episode that Jason watched in bits and pieces from the window of a classroom overlooking the Derwent River.

Jason knew that the Race School's annual Sponsors' Event was renowned for its carnival atmosphere, but he hadn't been prepared for the sheer *opulence* of that atmosphere.

The whole of the river had been decorated with flags and banners. Hover boats happily tooted their horns, welcoming the flotilla of yachts and hover vessels that descended upon Hobart.

Around lunchtime, *gigantic* hover yachts began to arrive at the Royal Hobart Yacht Club. They variously belonged to famous movie stars, visiting politicians, and of course the heads of the major hover car manufacturers and race teams. One wholly chartered hover liner pulled into the main dock and unloaded a bevy of glamorously dressed women and powerfully dressed men, the elite of Europe and America's East Coast.

Last and most celebrated of all came the professional racers who had once been students at the Race School.

La Bomba Romba, from Italy.

Fabian, from France.

And Angus Carver, the fighter pilot and member of the elite U.S. Air Force Racing Team.

It was celebrity heaven. The local media just loved it.

Jason, however, didn't really get it.

As far as he was concerned, the Sponsors' Event was about winning a knockout tournament. But for all of these people, it seemed to be just as much about attending the school's black-tie Gala Ball that evening and the

Victory Dinner on the Saturday evening after the tournament, doing deals, and *being seen* at every marquee in between. Apparently, the Sponsors' Event was one of the big events on the global "society calendar."

Jason didn't even know what a society calendar was.

And then, around midafternoon—to the media's absolute delight—the largest private yacht of all arrived, bearing a royal insignia on its bow.

The crest of the Royal Family of Monesi.

Prince Xavier's father, King Francis of Monesi, had come to watch his eldest son compete in the tournament.

And while all this was happening, Jason, the Bug, and Sally went to class: Jason and the Bug—overseen by Scott Syracuse—did simulator sessions on virtual tracks that featured demag strips.

At the same time, Sally was busy erecting two closed-circuit cameras in their pit bay—pit practice was next and Syracuse, feeling that the *Argonaut*'s pit stops had been somewhat erratic over the course of the season, wanted

The largest private yacht of all arrived.

Sally to see for herself exactly what she was doing before, during, and after each stop.

Curiously, both Horatio Wong and Isaiah Washington were once again too sick to attend classes.

Jason suspected they were faking it in an effort to get some relaxation time before the big day. Both Wong and Washington had qualified for the tournament, and strangely when they had been "ill" in the past, they had raced just fine the following day.

For his part, Syracuse barely raised an eyebrow when he got the call from the school nurse about their illnesses. He just went on with his classes.

And in a funny way, Jason felt that Syracuse was treating Team *Argonaut* with more respect than his other two teams simply *because* they came to class, even when they were obviously weary. It was as if just by keeping up with their mentor's tough schedule they were earning respect in Syracuse's eyes.

Jason and the Bug were to meet their parents during lunch, but when they got to the riverside park where they had agreed to meet, only Henry Chaser was there.

"Where's Mom?" Jason asked.

"Said she had some knitting or something to do," Henry replied. "Don't know what's got into her head, but when we got home last night, she pulled out her sewing kit and worked halfway into the night on something."

"Oh, okay . . ."

For the rest of their lunch hour, Jason, the Bug, and Henry watched the hover vessels gather on the river, munching on sandwiches.

Then it was back to class, to the afternoon's pit practice.

It was perhaps their most grueling practice session yet, with Syracuse working them hard—and all of it watched by the two all-seeing closed-circuit cameras.

Syracuse even had them practice an almost archaic form of pit stop: the manual stop, a stop during which all electric power in the pit bay had failed, meaning that Sally had to attach all six magneto drives to the *Argonaut* manually.

It was the Bug who figured out how to make such a stop happen faster: When he saw Sally struggling, he jumped out of the cockpit and helped her.

When he saw this, Scott Syracuse actually clapped. "Navigator! Excellent thinking! You don't see manual stops much these days, but they *can* occur. Just because the power's out doesn't mean the race is off. And that's how you handle them: You just get out of your car and you help your mech chief. Good thinking, Mr. Bug."

The Bug beamed with pride.

Every few stops, they would crowd around the TV monitors and watch the feed from the cameras. Sally frowned as she watched herself. "Look at that, I'm all over the shop. Spent mags here, new coolant there, compressed-air cylinders all over the place. My God, I never knew . . ."

Syracuse nodded. "I can tell you and tell you what you have to do, but sometimes you just need to see for yourself."

Then, at exactly 4 P.M.—two hours earlier than usual—Syracuse called an end to the session. "Great work today, people. Grab a drink and take a seat."

They did so and, utterly exhausted, fell into their chairs.

The thing was, Syracuse still wasn't finished.

He put up a spreadsheet on the vid-screen. "This just came in. It's the draw for tomorrow. Fourteen starters, rankings based on each racer's current position in the Championship Standings."

Jason gazed up at the tournament draw. It looked like the draw for a tennis tournament:

ROUND 1	QRTR FINALS	SEMI FINALS	FINAL
1. XONORA, X.			
16. [BYE]	1. XONORA, X.		
10. LUCAS, L.			
8. WONG, H.			
6. CORTEZ, J.			
11. PHAROS, A.			
14. MORIALTA, R.			
4. KRISHNA, V.			
3. WASHINGTON, I.			
13. TAKESHI, T.			
12. CHASER, J.			
5. PIPER, A.			
7. DIXON, W.			
9. SCHUMACHER, K.			
15. [BYE]	2. BECKER, B.		
2. BECKER, B.			

Jason saw himself in the bottom half of the draw. His first race would be against . . .

Oh, no.

Ariel Piper.

His opening race would be against his only friend at the Race School. What was the old saying: "There are no friends on the track."

In any case, with Ariel, Barnaby Becker, and Isaiah Washington all in his half of the draw, it struck Jason that the lower half was easily the tougher side of the draw.

It was with great disgust that he noticed that both Prince Xavier and Barnaby Becker had scored byes through the first round. Since there were only fourteen racers in the draw, the top two-ranked racers got the benefit of byes through the first round.

The format for the day was known as "short-course match racing": Two cars raced inside a walled track shaped in a tight figure-8. You won the match race in one of two ways: first, by lapping your opponent; or second, if neither racer could lap his opponent, by being the first to cross the Start-Finish Line after 100 laps. Since it was a short course—taking about 30 seconds to get around—100 laps would take about 50 minutes.

"So," Syracuse said. "Any questions about tomorrow?"

That took Jason by surprise.

It was the first time he could remember Syracuse offering specific advice about an impending race.

"Sure. What's the secret to short-course match racing?"

"You do get right to the point, don't you, Mr. Chaser?" Syracuse mused. "What's the secret to match racing? How about this: *Never give up. Never say die.* No matter how hopeless your situation appears to be, don't throw in the towel. Some racers go to pieces when something goes wrong and they find their opponent hammering on their tailfin. They just fold and let the other guy by, thus losing the race. Never *ever* do that. Because you don't know what problems *he's* got under his bonnet. You might throw in the race two seconds before he was going to pit."

"What about pit stops then?" Sally asked.

"Gotta be fast in match racing," Syracuse said. "When each lap is only 30 seconds long, you can't afford anything longer than a 15-second stop. Any longer and your opponent will be all over you when you come out. Then you're only one mistake away from defeat."

The Bug whispered something to Jason.

Jason said: "The Bug wants to know your ideas on *when* to pit. Early? Late? First or always second, like they say in the textbooks?"

"The pits are the X-factor in match racing," Syracuse said, "because whenever you stop your car, you run the risk of it not starting up again. Many a racer has pulled into the pits in a match race and never come out again, only to watch helplessly as his rival cruises around the track to an easy victory. That's why the books advocate pitting second. I agree. It's also why I wanted you guys to drill pit sessions today."

He looked over at Sally. "Pit action becomes even more crucial the longer a match race goes on—you might have to make decisions about whether to do a full-service stop or just a mag change. The key is to be out on the track. As long as you're out there, even if you're racing on one mag, you can still win. *Never* give up. *Never* say die. But then," he turned to Jason, "from what I've observed so far this season, Mr. Chaser, I can't see that being a problem for you."

THE GRAND BALLROOM
THE WALDORF HOTEL, HOBART

It looked like something out of a fairy tale.

The theme for the evening was "Among the Clouds," so the entire Grand Ballroom of the Waldorf was filled with 80-foot-high blue sails and fluffy machine-generated clouds. The effect was startling—you felt as if you were dining high in the sky, literally among the clouds.

Jason Chaser entered the great ballroom wearing a hand-me-down tuxedo. Beside him, the Bug and Henry Chaser wore regular suits and ties—they didn't have tuxedos, so they just wore the best outfits they had. Sally McDuff wore a shiny sky-blue dress that brought out the very best in her busty frame. Martha Chaser continued her peculiar behavior and did not attend, insisting that she had "things to do" back in the trailer.

The ballroom before them was filled with wealthy and famous people wearing the best outfits money could buy. Men in designer dinner suits, women in custom-made Valentinos, dripping with jewels.

Famous racers were spread around the room: Over in the corner was the reigning world champion, Alessandro Romba; by the bar, the American air force pilot, Carver. And at a table near the stage, talking with King Francis and Xavier Xonora, was the much-reviled French racer, Fabian—the villain of the pro circuit: cunning, brilliant, and utterly ruthless, and also totally at ease being universally despised by every race fan outside France.

"Hey! Jason!"

Jason turned and saw Ariel Piper—looking absolutely sensational in a figure-hugging silver gown—coming toward him.

"My, don't you clean up well . . . ," Ariel said, eyeing Jason's tux. "Although not as well as your dashing little navigator here," she winked sexily at the Bug, who flushed bright pink.

"I thought you ran a great race yesterday, Jason," she said. "Gutsy stuff skipping your last stop."

"I had to win," Jason said simply.

"And so do I in the first round tomorrow, buddy," Ariel said. "What is it they say: There are no friends on the track. I'm not going to cut you any slack tomorrow, Jason. I just wanted you to know that."

Jason nodded. "Don't worry, I'll be racing as hard as I can too."

"So we'll still be friends afterward?" Ariel said, genuinely concerned. And as he saw the look on her face, Jason realized that Ariel Piper had probably lost friends in the past after beating them in hover car races.

He smiled at her. "Sure." Then he added mischievously: "Of course, that's assuming you're not too devastated when I beat you."

Ariel broke out in a wide grin. "Oh, you nervy little man! I'll see you out on the track!"

An absolute bear of a man

And with that she danced off to her table.

Jason and his team went to theirs.

Scott Syracuse was already seated there when they arrived.

"Hello, Jason, Henry, Bug," Syracuse said, standing. "A tad different from our dinner last night?"

"Just a bit," Henry Chaser said. A simple hard-working man, he was a little intimidated by the wealth and power on display that night. It made him awkward, unsure of how to act in such company. "Somehow, I don't think they'll be serving takeout burgers here."

"If that is what you want, then that is what we shall have!" an Italian voice boomed from behind him.

Henry, Jason, and the Bug all whirled around.

Standing behind them was an absolute bear of a man dressed in an expensive dinner suit that struggled to contain his enormous belly. His wobbly jowls were covered by a black beard that was impeccably trimmed.

Jason recognized the man instantly, and his jaw involuntarily dropped.

"Umberto Lombardi," Syracuse said, "allow me to introduce to you Jason Chaser, his father, Henry, and his brother and navigator, the Bug."

Syracuse turned to Jason. "Umberto is an old friend of mine, and when we met earlier, I asked him if he would stop by our table later in the evening, but he insisted on joining us for the whole dinner."

Jason was still flabbergasted.

Umberto Lombardi was the billionaire owner of the Lombardi Racing Team, one of the few privately owned pro-racing teams.

Lombardi was an Italian property developer who'd made his fortune with the outrageously successful Venice II project. When he'd proposed the idea of *rebuilding* Venice fifty miles to the east of the original city—an exact replica, complete with crystal-clear chlorinated canals—and equipping it with ultramodern apartments, he had been laughed off as a lunatic.

But as the development proceeded and people saw Lombardi's vision take its wonderful form, the apartments quickly sold out—mainly to playboy race car drivers and the rich and famous of Europe.

Venice II became the hottest address in the world. Venice III quickly followed—where else, but in Venice Beach, California—and then came Venice IV, V, and VI.

But Lombardi's passion was hover car racing, and this larger-than-life fellow had become the pleasant oddity of the racing world. Even when his team came in dead last in the championship, he still happily threw money at it. He was known as a finder of new talent— talent that was quickly poached by the big-paying manufacturer teams.

"You know," Lombardi boomed, taking his seat between Jason and Henry Chaser, "these gala dinners can be so *stuffy* sometimes. Caviar, truffles, foie gras. Bah! Honestly, sometimes all I want is a good hearty cheese-burger!" He nudged Jason with his elbow. "Don't worry, my young friend. If the food stinks, we'll get some pizza delivered. That'll give these social parasites something to gossip about at their next dinner party."

Jason smiled. He liked Umberto Lombardi.

It was then that Lombardi—giant loud Umberto Lombardi—saw the Bug sitting on the other side of Jason, eyes wide, almost cowering behind his brother.

"And who do we have here!" Lombardi boomed, delighted. "My, you are a little fellow to be flying around in an aerial bullet. . . ."

From that moment, the Gala Dinner went swimmingly.

The night went quickly for Jason.

Umberto Lombardi was the best dinner companion he'd ever encountered. The man talked about racing and building property developments, meeting movie stars, and even how he'd been the first person to give Scott Syracuse a start in the pros.

But if nothing else, Jason learned that night that hover car racing wasn't just done on the track. The *business* of racing was done at dinners like this.

Jean-Pierre LeClerq made a speech, flanked by banners covered with the logos of all the school's sponsors. And Jason realized what sponsorship was all about—recognition. As LeClerq was doing now in front of some of the most influential people in the world, you always mentioned your sponsors.

After the speeches were over, the diners spread out around the room.

At one point, as Jason left his table to go to the men's room, he saw Ariel Piper standing at the bar, looking beautiful in her sleek silver dress—but also looking very awkward, seemingly trapped there by a tall guy in his twenties with slicked-back hair and a pointed hawkish nose. The bow tie of his expensive tux was loosened, and he was stroking Ariel's chin slowly with his index finger.

"Hey, Ariel." Jason came over. "How's it going? Hi," he said to the man in the tux. It took Jason a moment to realize that he knew who this fellow was—he was Fabian, the infamous French hover car racer.

"Jason, please—" Ariel said.

"Beat it, kid," Fabian snarled. "Can't you see we're busy here." His French-accented voice was slurred, drunk.

Fabian turned back to Ariel. "Like I said, there could be opportunities in the racing world for a girl of your . . . er, talents. That is, of course, *if* you play your cards right. Consider my offer, and maybe I'll see you later."

And with that, he placed something in Ariel's hand and left.

Jason couldn't be sure what it was, but it looked like a hotel room cardkey.

Then he looked at Ariel: She was gripping the room key tightly in her fist and staring off after Fabian, as if she were making a big decision. Jason watched as a peculiar series of emotions crossed her face—calculation, revulsion, and *ambition*.

"Ariel. Are you okay?" he asked, concerned.

Ariel continued to gaze after Fabian. He had left the dining room now, walking in the direction of the elevators.

"Jason," she said, still looking away. "You're a nice guy and a good kid. But there are some things about the world you don't understand yet."

And gripping the room key, she strode off after Fabian.

Jason could only watch her go.

"I understand more than you know," he said to the empty air behind her.

At 10:30, Jason and the Bug took their leave of Umberto Lombardi and Scott Syracuse.

It was time to get to bed.

They had to race tomorrow.

THE SPONSORS'
TOURNAMENT:
SHORT-COURSE
MATCH-RACE FORMAT

══════ Course

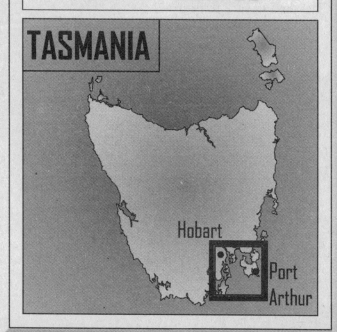

TASMANIA

Hobart

Port
Arthur

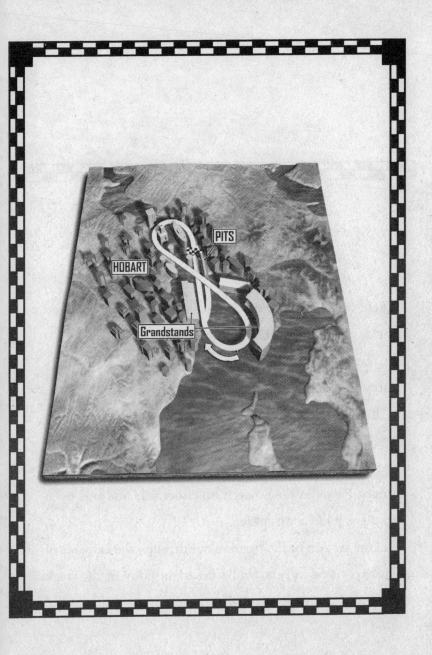

There was tension in the air as dawn came to Hobart on the day of the Sponsors' Tournament.

The rising sun glinted off a *gigantic* temporary structure that dominated the city.

It took the shape of a massive figure-8, with a single walled lane wide enough for two hover cars snaking its way around it. This "racelane" had walls of clear reinforced Plexiglas bounding it on either side and was open to the sky like a rat maze.

One section of the figure-8 cut through the canyons of Hobart's skyscrapers, while the main body of the track extended out over Storm Bay, where it was surrounded by immense grandstands, floodlight towers, and, today, an ESPN television blimp. In fact, today there were TV cameras everywhere, as the tournament was to be broadcast on racing channels around the world.

The crowds had come out in force: 250,000 people in the stands alone, while experienced locals watched the city section of the track from rooftops and open office windows.

Jason, the Bug, and Sally arrived in Pit Lane at 7:30 A.M. to find the area bustling with activity. Jason noticed right away that quite a few of the other teams wore brand-new team uniforms, their cars and even their racing boots spit-polished for their big day in front of the international sponsors.

And suddenly Jason felt self-conscious in his race clothes: his old denim overalls, workboots, and his battle-scarred motorcycle helmet.

His father was supposed to be with them—he had wanted to experience the tension of Pit Lane with his boys—but at the last moment, Martha had stopped him, saying she needed him to help her with the strange project that had kept her locked away in her trailer the past day and a half.

The tension in the air was palpable.

This was no ordinary day's racing at the Race School. There was more than championship points at stake here. Careers could be made or lost today.

Then Jason saw Ariel in her pit bay and he waved. She saw him, but didn't return the gesture. Nor did she look him in the eye.

At 8:45 A.M., a televized ceremony in Pit Lane saw the drawing of the race order. Each first-round race was given a number and Jean-Pierre LeClerq drew the numbers out of a hat.

The first race of the day would be . . .

Chaser, Jason v. Piper, Ariel.

Their race was scheduled to start at 9:30 A.M., but before it was to take place, at 9 o'clock, there was scheduled a "Parade of Racers" in front of the main VIP Grandstand, situated on the Start-Finish Line. And as he looked at the slickly uniformed teams around him, suddenly Jason didn't feel like being "presented" to the assembled sponsors in his old denims.

But he had no choice.

And so the Parade of Racers proceeded, and he stood there in front of the world, flanked by flags and banners and with the TV blimp soaring in the sky above him, in his crappy denims . . . and he had never felt more embarrassed in his life. He hated every minute of it.

Then, mercifully, the parade ended, the crowd roared, and the track was cleared for the first race of the day.

Sally prepped the *Argonaut* and the Tarantula.

The Bug worked on pit schedule strategies—in between peering fearfully at the packed grandstands outside.

Jason just sat on his own, centering himself, preparing to race.

The clock ticked over to 9:20 and a loudspeaker boomed with the race director's voice: "*Would racers Chaser and Piper please take their positions on the track! Five minutes to racetime . . .*"

Jason got to his feet—

—just as his parents, both of them, ran into the pit area, his mother calling, "Jason! Doodlebug! Wait!"

She carried a large laundry bag in her hands.

Breathless, she arrived at Team *Argonaut*'s pit bay.

"Mom!" Jason said. "What is it?"

"I'm sorry I couldn't get them done sooner," Martha Chaser said, still puffing. She opened the laundry bag—

—to reveal a beautiful set of leather racing uniforms.

Blue.

Silver.

And white.

The colors of the *Argonaut*.

They were full-body uniforms, with the gloves and racing boots seamlessly attached. And the design was *cool*. Mainly white, it looked as if the wearer of the uniform had dipped his arms and legs in blue paint—and, as a nice touch, the blue sections were edged with sparkling silver. Each bore the number 55 on the left-hand shoulder.

There was one uniform for Jason.

A smaller one for the Bug.

And a third one . . . for Sally McDuff.

Martha handed Sally hers: "I made sure yours has a little extra support in the chest, dear."

And then Henry Chaser pulled out his surprise: two medium-sized boxes with SHOEI written on the outside.

"No way . . . ," Jason said.

He opened his box, and extracted from it a brand-new navy-blue Shoei racing helmet.

The Bug also got one, although his was white. And since she didn't need a helmet, Sally got a blue baseball cap with ARGONAUT 55 embroidered on it.

Martha said, "After I watched you all win together on Thursday, the only thing I could think of was: what a great team. But every great team needs to *look* like one. So I got some material, bought some race car magazines to check the current styles, and spent the last day-and-a-half determined to make you look like a team."

Jason gave her a big hug. So did the Bug. "Thanks, Mom!"

Team Argonaut strode out.

"Come on, boys," Henry Chaser said. "Better get into those suits! You've got a race to win."

A few minutes later, Team *Argonaut* strode out onto the track, into the sunshine, in front of the roaring crowd, dressed in their spanking new racesuits, Shoei helmets dangling from their hands, eyes fixed, game faces on.

Ariel Piper's team were already on the track, waiting beside the *Pied Piper*.

"What is this? *The Right Stuff*? *Armageddon*?" Ariel's navigator said wryly.

Jason nodded to Ariel as he slid into the cockpit of the *Argonaut*.

"No friends on the track, Jason," Ariel said.

"Whatever you say, Ariel."

RACE 1:

CHASER V. PIPER

The two hover cars sat side by side on the grid, the *Argonaut* on the left, the *Pied Piper* on the right.

From his cockpit, all Jason could see was the wide glass-like corridor of Plexiglas stretching away from him before it banked steeply to the left into the forest of city buildings.

And then—*tone, tone, ping*—the start lights went green and the two cars shot off the mark and the crowds in the stands roared.

Two cars.

One enclosed track.

Hyperfast speeds.

Flashing sunshine.

Blurring walls.

The *Argonaut* and the *Pied Piper* banked and swerved as they rushed like a pair of bullets around the track, ducking and swooping and missing each other by inches as they jockeyed for position.

Out of the corner of his eye on his right side, Jason glimpsed the red-and-white nose of the *Pied Piper* shooting around the track alongside him.

After five quick laps, there was nothing in it.

After ten, they were still side by side.

Jason's concentration was hyperintense, eyeing the speed-blurred track whizzing by him.

Round and round they went, zipping over and under the figure-8 track, at some points side by side, at others on each other's heels, swapping the lead but never by more than a couple of car-lengths.

The crowd was captivated.

And then suddenly like a horse throwing a shoe, Jason unexpectedly lost a magneto drive and although more than

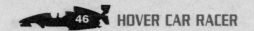

anything he didn't want to pit first, he peeled off into the pits.

Ariel stayed on the track, shooting off on the next 30-second lap.

The crowd gasped.

Jason had 30 seconds.

He hit the pit bay. The Tarantula descended.

7 seconds . . . 8 . . .

The *Pied Piper* zoomed through the city section.

New mags went on. A splash of coolant.

The *Pied Piper* zoomed over the crossover of the figure-8.

13 seconds . . . 14 seconds.

"Sally . . . !"

"Almost done . . . okay! *Go!*"

And Sally cut short the stop and the Tarantula withdrew into the ceiling and Jason hit the gas and blasted out of the pits *just as* Ariel came screaming round the final turn, hard on the *Argonaut*'s heels—now only several carlengths behind it!

This was classic match racing, the part of the race known as the "chase phase."

The *Pied Piper* (no pit stops) was hammering on the tail of the *Argonaut* (one stop), chasing it down. If Jason made even the slightest mistake and Ariel got her nose a fraction of an inch ahead of him, it was race over.

And it only had to be a fraction of an inch— microchips attached to nosewings of both cars would start screaming as soon as they detected one car to be a lap ahead of the other.

Jason had to hold Ariel off until she was forced to pit.

But she didn't pit.

She just kept chasing him.

Charging after him.

Hunting him down, taking each banking turn perfectly, gaining with each lap. Hauling him in foot by brutal foot.

After one lap, she was two car-lengths behind the *Argonaut*.

After two: one car-length.

And after three laps, she had crept *inside* a car-length!

It was relentless. Ariel was throwing everything at him,

taking every turn cleanly, searching for a way past him, giving him the race of her life.

On the fourth such lap, Jason's lead became half a car-length.

Hold your nerve . . . , he told himself. *Hold your nerve. . . .*

Five laps. Most chase phases ended around the fifth lap, with either the pursuer pitting, or the runner crashing out.

Six laps.

And Ariel came alongside him!

She's trying to force you into an error.

Seven laps.

Now it was side-by-side racing!

Jason kept his eyes fixed forward—if he dared to look sideways, he imagined he could see Ariel's eyes inside her racing helmet.

Eight laps, and the crowd rose to their feet.

Eight laps! Jason's mind screamed. *How long is she going to keep this up? When is she going to pit!*

Then on the ninth lap of the chase, he saw the *Pied Piper*'s red-and-white nosewing creep into his peripheral vision.

No! She's gonna take me!

The crowds started cheering.

Never give up. Never say die.

And as they roared down the main straightaway, commencing Lap 20—the tenth lap of the chase phase—Ariel peeled off and vanished into the pits.

The crowd burst into applause—Jason had just survived a nine-lap chase, almost double the average. An incredible feat of concentration under pressure.

And with Ariel finally off his tail, he gunned it.

Ariel's pit stop was near perfect, and she came back out onto the track slightly ahead of Jason, but now on the same lap.

Lap 40 went by—and there was nothing in it.

Another chase phase took place between Laps 50 and 55, but Jason survived that.

Around Lap 81, Jason had his own chase phase, but Ariel fended him off determinedly.

Then Ariel tried again when Jason pitted on Lap 90, but there was no dice there.

Which meant that after 96 laps and 48 minutes of superb match racing, it was now a flat-out dash for the line over the last four laps.

The two cars whipped round the track, banking with the corners like a pair of missiles, matching streaks of blue and red.

With three laps to go, Jason was exhausted, his nerves and reflexes stretched to the limit. He didn't know if he could keep this up.

Two laps to go, and his eyes began to blur . . . and Ariel crept ahead of him.

60 seconds of racing left.

Into the city section, and Jason jammed his thrusters all the way forward.

The *Argonaut* roared across the overpass and rocketed into the right-hander at almost 90 degrees to the earth and in doing so gained a yard on the *Pied Piper*.

The two cars screamed out of the final turn, commencing the last lap, the *Pied Piper* less than a yard in front.

Jason clenched his teeth. Gunned it.

His head was beginning to spin.

And the winner was . . .

Through the city buildings, banking hard—the *Pied Piper* just a red shape ahead of him—the roar of the crowd invading his thoughts.

Over the crossover and toward the final right-hander, all pedals and levers and dials in the red. And then, in a fleeting split-second instant, Jason saw it.

Saw Ariel make a mistake.

She was taking the last turn too wide. The very last turn—the 200th corner of this nerve-shattering, reflex-burning race.

And so, calling on his last reserves of energy and skill, Jason pounced.

He started the turn wide and cut sharply *inside* Ariel—

—and as they took the turn together, the *Argonaut* swooped inside the *Pied Piper* . . .

. . . and came fully alongside it . . .

. . . and the two cars shoomed down the final straightaway together, and after 100 laps of the most intense match racing imaginable they crossed the Finish Line almost perfectly side by side and the winner was—

—the *Argonaut*.

By the tip of its nosewing.

The official winning margin, taken from the microchips on the nosewings of the two cars, would later be recorded as 0.04 of a second—four hundredths of a second—in favor of "Chaser, J."

Physically exhausted and emotionally spent, Jason returned to the pits.

Around him the tournament continued apace; the next pair of racers already lining up on the grid, getting ready to go.

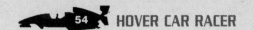

The *Argonaut* slid into its bay—steaming—the acrid smell of overheated magneto drives wafting through the air all around it.

Jason and the Bug stepped out, removed their helmets from their sweaty heads—to be at once embraced in the arms of Sally McDuff and their proud parents.

"You are one gutsy little racer, Jason Chaser!" Sally exclaimed. "I thought she had you in that first chase phase."

"Me, too!" Henry said. "Nine laps! You held her off for nine laps! I've never seen anything like it! How did you do it?"

Jason offered a wry glance to Scott Syracuse, standing nearby: "Never give up. Never say die."

With that, Jason's parents let him be, allowing him and the Bug to slump into their chairs in the rear corner of their pit bay.

Syracuse came over. Looked at Jason and the Bug, exhausted, their hair all sweaty and tousled.

And he smiled.

"Nice racing, boys," he said. "Very nice. I haven't seen

a racer hold his nerve like that for a very long time, Mr. Chaser."

"Thank you, sir," Jason said.

"Now take a shower and get some rest, both of you. The next round will be here faster than you know and you want to be fresh for it."

Jason emerged from the showers of his pit bay ten minutes later—just in time to see Ariel over in her pit bay, talking animatedly to Fabian.

Well, in actual fact, only she was talking.

He was walking away, dismissing her tearful pleas with a curt wave of his hand.

Fabian strode off, leaving Ariel standing there in her pit bay, alone, tears streaming down her face.

Jason knew what was going on. Ariel had gone to Fabian's room the night before—he didn't want to think about what happened there—and now she'd lost in the opening round of the tournament, and suddenly Fabian didn't want to know her.

As he gazed at her now, Jason felt for Ariel. She'd given Fabian something last night, something of herself, and for all the wrong reasons, but Fabian had only been using her—

But then Ariel turned suddenly, and caught Jason staring.

And the two of them stood there, on opposite sides of the pits, just looking at each other.

Jason didn't break eye contact. Nor was he going to. It was Ariel who turned away and disappeared into her pit bay.

"I'm sorry, Ariel," Jason whispered to no one. "But there are no friends on the track."

The tournament continued apace, its carnival-like atmosphere pumping. In between races there were pop music acts, while in the VIP marquees, sponsors and Race School officials did deals over flutes of Moët champagne.

Of the six first-round races, Jason and Ariel's had easily been the longest. The others had been quicker, less-intense affairs, and had variously been won through crashes or mishaps in the pits. None of them had even come close to reaching the 50-lap mark, let alone 100.

And so with the completion of the first round, the tournament draw looked like this:

ROUND 1	QRTR FINALS	SEMI FINALS	FINAL
1. XONORA, X.			
16. [BYE]	1. XONORA, X.		
10. LUCAS, L.	8. WONG, H.		
8. WONG, H.			
6. CORTEZ, J.			
11. PHAROS, A.	6. CORTEZ, J.		
14. MORIALTA, R.	4. KRISHNA, V.		
4. KRISHNA, V.			
3. WASHINGTON, I.			
13. TAKESHI, T.	3. WASHINGTON, I.		
12. CHASER, J.	12. CHASER, J.		
5. PIPER, A.			
7. DIXON, W.			
9. SCHUMACHER, K.	9. SCHUMACHER, K.		
15. [BYE]	2. BECKER, B.		
2. BECKER, B.			

The second round—the Quarter Final Round—promised some interesting races and it didn't disappoint.

1ST QUARTER FINAL:

XONORA V. WONG

The opening race of the Quarter Final Round saw the first appearance of the top seed, Xavier Xonora, and he showed everyone exactly why he was the favorite to win the tournament.

Up against Jason's stablemate, Horatio Wong, Xonora was quite simply merciless.

His driving around the figure-8 circuit was faultless. He didn't take a corner more than an inch off the optimum racing line and within eight laps, he was a full third of a lap ahead of Wong.

Then Wong pitted—a huge tactical mistake, the Bug

commented to Jason; you never *ever* pitted when you were that far behind—and suddenly Xavier was all over him like a rash.

The all-black *Speed Razor* loomed behind Wong's car like a giant hawk—while Wong swerved defensively, panicking, wrestling with his steering wheel.

Xavier made a couple of lazy feints to the left, before he just powered easily by Wong on the final turn of Lap 11, overtaking him on the inside, and the race was over almost before it had begun.

It was the shortest race so far. Some likened it to a chess expert dispatching a novice in five quick moves. Others said it was nothing less than the clinical *execution* of a lesser racer by a master.

It even seized the attention of the assembled sponsors.

Xavier Xonora was good, very good. And he had charged into the semis without even breaking a sweat.

2ND QUARTER FINAL:

CORTEZ V. KRISHNA.

A tight and tense race between the gifted but unpredictable Mexican, Joaquin Cortez, and the No. 4 seed, a very gifted eighteen-year-old racer from India named Varishna Krishna.

It was ultimately won by Krishna on Lap 74, during the race's sixth chase phase.

3RD QUARTER FINAL:

SCHUMACHER V. BECKER

This was a race, all agreed, that illustrated the cruelty of match racing.

The German, Schumacher, had led all the way. He had been pitting superbly—consistently clocking astonishing 8-second stops—and rocketing around the track like a bullet.

By the 50-lap mark, he had built a solid half-lap lead on Becker and all the commentators were certain that after his next pit stop, on fresh mags, he'd pounce.

That pit stop, however, saw Schumacher's pit machine freeze in midair.

System crash.

And while Schumacher's mech chief swore and rebooted their pit machine's central processing unit, Barnaby Becker just whipped around the circuit—alone, on semidepleted mags—and lapped Schumacher in the easiest possible way, while he was still in the pits, thus taking a race that by all accounts he really didn't deserve to win.

But then, everyone said, that was match racing.

There was one more Quarter Final race to be run and the crowd murmured in anticipation.

The public knew that both racers studied under the same teacher at the Race School—which always made for interesting racing.

But everyone at the Race School knew that there was more to it than that: They all knew that Isaiah Washington despised his upstart young stablemate, Jason Chaser.

The stage was set.

The two cars lined up on the grid.

4TH QUARTER FINAL:

WASHINGTON V. CHASER

The race between Isaiah Washington and Jason was nothing short of electric.

More than any of the other races in the day so far, there was *feeling* in this one. The crowd sensed the tension in the air as the two cars lined up on the grid and Isaiah Washington glared over at Jason and the Bug.

And then they were off and the race was run at a blistering pace, with multiple lead changes and daring passing maneuvers from both racers that had the crowd gasping.

After 20 laps, neither one had a clear lead. They were going stop for stop.

40 laps, and at the Bug's urging, Jason skipped a stop and tried a quick three-lap chase—but Washington held them off determinedly before embarking on a chase phase of his own, but that also failed.

Then, on Lap 57, a mistake.

In this pressure-cooker environment, it was only a matter of time before someone made a mistake and it was the most unexpected person of all who made it.

Sally McDuff.

It was an uncharacteristically rookie mistake, too—coordinating her pit gear, Sally mixed up her supply of old and new mag drives and she accidentally attached a *used* magneto drive to the Tarantula in preparation for the *Argonaut*'s next pit stop.

The stop took place and Jason gunned it out of the pits . . . and immediately knew something was wrong. He didn't have full power.

It was a costly error.

Because it meant that the *Argonaut* had to pit *again* on the very next lap.

"Jason! I'm so sorry!" Sally said as the Tarantula replaced the dud mag. "It's my fault!"

"Don't worry about it! Just get us back out there!" Jason yelled.

The old mag came off and the new one went on and Jason blasted out of the pits—

—and suddenly found himself only inches in front of the ravenous *Black Bullet*. He was almost a full lap behind now and flying for his life: Washington was on fresh mags, a full tank of coolant, and—according to the Bug—his eyes were deadly.

But Jason held on. Drove hard. Concentrated grimly.

That first chase phase melded into a second, then a third, then a fourth. In each instance, Jason could only pit *after* Washington did: in his position, to pit first was to concede defeat.

Never give up. Never say die . . .

Lap 82 saw Washington pit again—and not a moment too soon for Jason. The *Argonaut* had been almost out of coolant, its mags all but on the point of burning up.

Jason charged into the pits on the next lap for a full coolant refill.

And suddenly his luck changed.

Isaiah Washington was still in the pits when he got there.

Washington's pit machine had frozen halfway through attaching a new set of mags to his car and Washington's mech chief was now frantically trying to manually pull the machine clear of the *Black Bullet*.

Jason recalled the words of Scott Syracuse from a few days ago: "The pits are the X-factor in match racing, because whenever you stop your car, you run the risk of it not starting up again."

Which meant that Jason had now reclaimed the lap he had lost earlier—they were now on the same lap.

Jason flung the *Argonaut* into its pit bay—to find that Sally, rattled by her previous error, had misheard the Bug's radio instructions for a full coolant refill.

She had only prepared a top-up.

"Oh, Jason! I'm sorry!"

"Just give me what you've got!" Jason yelled. "We gotta go!"

The Tarantula's coolant hose pumped a small amount of oily green liquid into the *Argonaut*'s tank and Jason sped off . . .

. . . leaving Washington *still* in his pit bay.

The *Argonaut* shoomed around the track at bullet speed. Alone.

It had made almost one full circuit when the *Black Bullet* blasted out of the pits—in the nick of time—resuming its place on the track just as Jason rounded the final turn.

And abruptly the tables were turned.

Whereas Washington had spent much of this race hammering on Jason's tail, now—with only 16 laps to go—it was Jason who was almost a lap ahead, and it was his turn to do the hounding.

And despite his own exhaustion, that's exactly what Jason did.

For the next six laps, he rode the tail of the *Black*

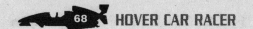

Bullet, harrying it, hassling it, creeping alongside it until their nosewings were almost side by side.

It was all Isaiah Washington could do to stay in front.

But then the Bug issued a warning.

The *Argonaut*'s coolant levels were dangerously low, which meant that its magneto drive heat levels were dangerously high.

Sally's top-up hadn't been enough. It wasn't going to get them to the end of the race. They were going to have to pit one more time, something that would sap the lead they'd just gained and make this race a dash to the finish.

The thing was, Jason was wiped, exhausted from all the previous chases—and he knew it. He didn't think he had the mental energy for another dash to the line.

"Ahhh!" he yelled. "I just can't do it!"

And then all of a sudden, at the end of Lap 90, something very unexpected happened.

Just as Jason was about to give up on his chase and peel away into the pits and kiss the race good-bye . . .

. . . Isaiah Washington gave up.

Worn out by Jason's brutal six-lap chase—and completely unaware of Jason's own coolant problems—Washington pulled into the pits, allowing the *Argonaut* to cruise by him, thus winning the match race.

The crowd cheered.

Jason was stunned.

The overwhelming fatigue that had gripped him moments ago was suddenly transformed into shock.

He had just won this race.

He had just made it to the semi finals.

The *Argonaut* returned to the pits, its mags practically smoking.

Sally McDuff came running over and hugged both Jason and the Bug in their seats. She apologized profusely, but Jason wouldn't hear any of it.

"Sally," he said. "Forget it. I've made far more mistakes out on the track than you have in here, and you've always covered for me. Hey. We win as a team and we lose as a team. Don't even think about it again."

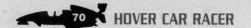

A few minutes later Isaiah Washington came over to their pit bay, with Scott Syracuse by his side. And to Jason's surprise, Washington extended his hand.

"Good race, Chaser," he said, shaking Jason's hand.

"You too."

At which point, Washington glanced at the Tarantula and saw the computer readout of the *Argonaut*'s mag and coolant levels. They were all deep into the red, bordering on blowout.

Washington's jaw dropped. "Wait a minute. You were redlining on coolant *and* mag levels when I dropped out?"

"Er, yeah."

"But . . . ," Washington stammered. "God, no . . . you were running on empty." But then his gaze became steely, suspicious. "How'd you learn to do that?"

Jason shrugged. "Mr. Syracuse taught us. Yesterday, in class."

"And what exactly did he say?" Washington demanded.

Jason let Syracuse answer that.

"Never give up," their teacher said.

• • •

Washington extended his hand.

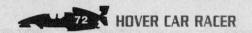

And so by midafternoon on Tournament Day, it was time for the semi finals and the tournament draw looked like this:

ROUND 1	QRTR FINALS	SEMI FINALS	FINAL
1. XONORA, X.			
16. [BYE]	1. XONORA, X.		
10. LUCAS, L.	8. WONG, H.	1. XONORA, X.	
8. WONG, H.			
6. CORTEZ, J.			
11. PHAROS, A.		4. KRISHNA, V.	
14. MORIALTA, R.	6. CORTEZ, J.		
4. KRISHNA, V.	4. KRISHNA, V.		
3. WASHINGTON, I.			
13. TAKESHI, T.	3. WASHINGTON, I.		
12. CHASER, J.	12. CHASER, J.	12. CHASER, J.	
5. PIPER, A.			
7. DIXON, W.			
9. SCHUMACHER, K.		2. BECKER, B.	
15. [BYE]	9. SCHUMACHER, K.		
2. BECKER, B.	2. BECKER, B.		

It was now the business end of the tournament.

It was time for some serious racing.

It was time for the semi finals.

1ST SEMI FINAL:

XONORA V. KRISHNA

If Xavier Xonora's first race in the tournament had been an 11-lap execution, then his semi final against Varishna Krishna was a slightly longer demolition.

It lasted all of 14 laps.

For on Krishna's first pit stop on Lap 10, the young Indian discovered that he'd received two depleted mags. A hurried second pit stop had ensued on the following lap, but by then Krishna's race was over.

Xavier Xonora didn't let mishaps like that go unpunished. Within four laps, he'd shot by Krishna and ended the race, putting the talented Indian racer out of his misery.

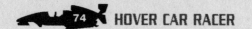

And so, having raced only 25 laps in the course of the tournament—all of 12 minutes' racing time—the Black Prince was in the final.

The next race between Jason Chaser and Barnaby Becker would determine who would face him.

"It's over *already*?" Jason said in disbelief.

He had only just stepped out of the shower at the rear of his pit bay, wrapped in a towel, when he was met by Sally McDuff and the news that Xavier Xonora had already beaten Varishna Krishna and that they were due on the grid in ten minutes.

"What happened to Krishna?" he asked. "Xavier's good, but he's not that good. Krishna's too talented a racer to go down in fourteen laps."

"Looks like Krishna got some bad mags," Sally said. "The mystery mag-demon strikes again. Hurry up, champ. We're on."

Jason grabbed his race suit. "Geez, I'm still just recovering from the last race."

• • •

The two hover cars sat on the grid, surrounded by their mech chiefs, mentors, and supporters.

Jason looked over at Barnaby Becker's maroon-colored Lockheed. Xavier Xonora, fresh from his semi final win over Varishna Krishna, was giving the helmeted Barnaby some tips, while Zoroastro simply glared directly at Jason, trying to psych him out.

"*Racers! This is your five-minute warning! All crew members are to leave the track area immediately,*" Race Director Calder's voice echoed out over the stadium's speakers.

"Stay sharp," Sally said, slapping Jason's helmet. "Don't take your eyes off this guy. He's a slippery customer." She turned to the Bug and slapped his helmet too. "And you, you look after your brother, okay?"

The Bug gave her a brisk double-thumbs-up.

"Hey, Sally," Jason said meaningfully.

She turned. "Yeah?"

"We're gonna beat this guy in the pits."

"Dang straight," Sally said.

She made to leave—just as someone else arrived at the *Argonaut* and stopped her.

It was Varishna Krishna.

Dark-eyed and handsome, with smooth chocolate-brown skin, Krishna was a very polite and articulate young man. He was still wearing his sweat-stained racing uniform. He must have come straight from his car after losing to Xavier.

"Jason, Bug, Sally. Hello."

"Krishna?" Jason frowned. "What—"

"A word of advice, young Jason. As you may know, I experienced some magneto drive problems in my last race. Let me tell you what happened. Two of my mags were depleted when they went onto my car. However, my mech chief, Darius, had checked them all beforehand, and they were okay. Which means that at some point *during the race* my mags were drained of their power. After the race, we found this lying next to our mag storage case."

Krishna held up a small radiolike device the size of a child's lunchbox.

Jason knew what it was instantly.

It was a portable microwave transmitter. Often used as a backup radio by race teams, portable microwave transmitters were usually kept as far away from magneto drives as possible—for the simple reason that, if left on, they sapped mag drives of their power.

"I just thought I'd warn you," Krishna said, eyeing Barnaby, Xavier, and Zoroastro disapprovingly. "I can't prove anything, but Barnaby comes from the same stable as Xavier, and, well . . . let's just say it might be something your mech chief will want to keep an eye on."

Jason nodded. "Thanks, Krishna. I . . . I didn't know you cared."

Despite his recent loss, Krishna smiled and placed a hand on Jason's shoulder. "Oh, young Master Chaser, do not doubt the impact you have. I know you've had a hard time here at Race School. But know this: Some of us enjoy watching you race. You have this delightful habit of hanging on by your fingertips to the bitter end. I suppose I just realized that it was time you knew you had a friend."

And with that, Krishna turned and walked off.

2ND SEMI FINAL:

CHASER V. BECKER

As the *Argonaut* and the all-maroon *Devil's Chariot* had been sitting side by side on the grid, waiting for the start of their semi final, Barnaby Becker had called to Jason: "Hey, Chaser. Time to die."

Jason replied simply: "Shut up and race."

And race they did—in an absolutely brutal contest.

Full-tilt racing.

In a word, Jason raced like a demon. But Barnaby was up to the challenge and for the first 30 laps, it was more a battle of wills than a match race. The two of them raced almost side by side, taking every turn together, every straightaway, even pitting together.

Indeed, for the first 30 laps, neither of them even attempted a chase phase—which sent a message to the crowd: This was not a chase, it was a 100-lap race to the Finish Line.

In the end, the stalemate was broken in the pits.

At around the 30-lap mark, Sally McDuff lifted her game—and she started sending the *Argonaut* back onto the track, fully replenished, with 8-second stops and even a 7-second one, the first such stop of the day.

The result was a steadily increasing lead.

The *Argonaut* started to pull away from the *Devil's Chariot*—and by Lap 75, Jason was a full quarter of a lap ahead. And based on the run of the race so far, that would be a lead that Barnaby couldn't surmount.

It was on Lap 75, however—while Sally was busy watching Jason whip down the home straightaway—that a dark figure slipped into the *Argonaut*'s pit bay behind her and placed something beside her next set of fresh mags.

A microwave radio transmitter.

Sally never saw the intruder. By the time she turned around to prepare for the next stop, he was gone.

A few laps later the *Argonaut* pitted and then shot back out onto the track—where Jason quickly realized that at least two of his new mags were cactus.

"Dang it!" he yelled. "Not now!"

Furious, he had to pit again.

But Barnaby didn't.

And so as the *Argonaut* pulled into the pits, the *Devil's Chariot* swept past it, and all of a sudden, in the space of two laps, the lead was reversed—and with only 19 circuits of the course remaining, Barnaby Becker now held a commanding half-lap lead.

Sadly for Jason, that lead proved to be too big. Desperate and determined, he chased Barnaby all the way to the end, but to no avail.

Barnaby held his lead and after 100 hard-fought laps, he cruised over the Finish Line and claimed his place in the final.

Chaser v. Becker

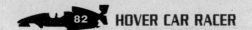

Jason could only punch his steering wheel with frustration and bring the *Argonaut* back to the pits.

His day was over.

He was out of the tournament.

The *Argonaut* returned to the pits—

—to find a large crowd gathered around its pit bay.

And this was no ordinary crowd either. It was a crowd of race officials and teachers, including the school's Race Director, Stanislaus Calder, the man in charge of the tournament, and Jean-Pierre LeClerq, making a rare visit from the VIP marquee.

And in the middle of this crowd stood Sally McDuff, with her arms folded, looking—of all things—pretty pleased with herself.

Jason stepped out of the *Argonaut*, frowning at the sight. He removed his helmet. Truth be told, after three energy-sapping races, he was tired as hell and he was looking forward to having a shower and a rest.

"Sally?" he said. "What's going on?"

Sally came over. "Don't put that helmet away, my talented young friend. We're not out of this tournament yet."

"What do you mean?"

"The judges are checking the video replay," Sally said enigmatically. "Come and see."

The race officials were indeed viewing two video monitors: The monitors that were connected to the two closed-circuit TV cameras hanging from the ceiling of the *Argonaut*'s pit bay; the monitors that Scott Syracuse had used during pit practice to allow Sally and the boys to see themselves in action.

On one monitor now was a clear black-and-white image of the *Argonaut*'s pit bay: It depicted Sally at work on the Tarantula during the semi final against Barnaby. A computer monitor on the Tarantula showed all the vital stats of the race so far, revealing that this was sometime around Lap 75, racetime 37:30 minutes.

Then Sally moved to the edge of the screen, looking out of the pit bay, and as she did so, a dark figure crept into the *Argonaut*'s pit bay behind her and quickly deposited a portable microwave transmitter next to her stack of magneto drives.

But as the dark figure sneaked away, he inadvertently glanced upward—looking directly into the camera—and everyone saw his face.

It was Guido Moralez.

Barnaby Becker's mech chief.

"Oh my Lord . . ." one of the race officials gasped.

The other School officials swapped shocked glances.

"Gentlemen!" Race Director Calder raised his voice above the murmurs. "By my order, an emergency hearing will be convened in ten minutes in the Race Briefing Room. Please advise Mr. Becker and his mech chief, Mr. Moralez, that their presence at this hearing is specifically requested. They have some questions to answer."

Thirty minutes later, the hearing was over.

In the face of Sally's damning video evidence of Moralez planting the microwave transmitter beside the *Argonaut*'s mag drives—thus depleting them of their power and forcing

Jason to pit again—Barnaby Becker had been disqualified from the tournament and his semi final victory quashed.

Race Director Calder had been particularly severe in his judgment.

He said that had it been entirely up to him, both Barnaby and Moralez would have been expelled from the Race School for such disgraceful conduct. But a plea from their teacher, Zoroastro—claiming that this was an act entirely out of character, a stupid act of desperation in the heat of racing—saved their bacon, and they merely had to suffer the indignity of being stripped of their victory.

And with the overturning of that victory came the announcement—an announcement that the 250,000-strong crowd greeted with delighted applause.

Jason and the *Argonaut* were now in the final.

Leaving the Race Briefing Room, Race Director Calder said to Jason: "Mr. Chaser. The final will commence in twenty minutes. See you on the grid."

"We'll be there, sir," Jason nodded.

As he strode back to the pits, Sally fell into step alongside him, grinning like a sphinx.

Jason eyed her sideways. "Why are you smiling like that?"

Sally just raised her eyebrows.

Jason said, "Now that I think about it, you never switched on those closed-circuit cameras for any of our other races in this tournament, did you?"

"Nope."

"But you switched them on for the semi?"

"I did. After what Krishna told us, I thought some precautions might be in order," she said. "Jason. You race these guys out on the track, but I also race them—in the pits. And I was determined to beat these losers in the pits. And I did. That was my best race yet, and I sure as hell wasn't gonna let anyone stiff us with some mysteriously depleted magneto drives."

Jason turned to face her as they walked. In her own way, Sally McDuff was just as proud and determined as he was.

He nodded to her. "You're a legend, Sally."

The next twenty minutes went by in a blur.

With the sun beginning to set, the gigantic track and the bay around it were bathed in a diffused orange glow. The floodlights came on.

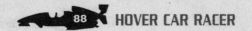

The crowds in the hovering grandstands were buzzing with excitement.

The tournament draw itself told the story of a great day's racing:

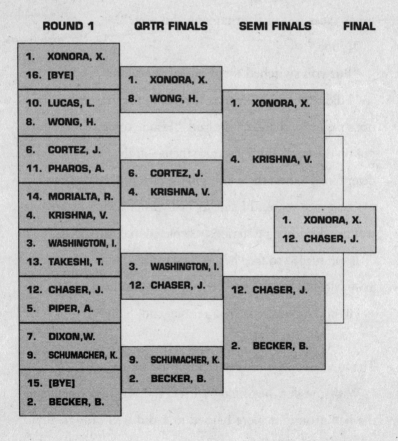

ROUND 1	QRTR FINALS	SEMI FINALS	FINAL
1. XONORA, X.			
16. [BYE]	1. XONORA, X.		
10. LUCAS, L.	8. WONG, H.	1. XONORA, X.	
8. WONG, H.			
6. CORTEZ, J.		4. KRISHNA, V.	
11. PHAROS, A.	6. CORTEZ, J.		
14. MORIALTA, R.	4. KRISHNA, V.		
4. KRISHNA, V.			1. XONORA, X.
3. WASHINGTON, I.			12. CHASER, J.
13. TAKESHI, T.	3. WASHINGTON, I.		
12. CHASER, J.	12. CHASER, J.	12. CHASER, J.	
5. PIPER, A.			
7. DIXON, W.		2. BECKER, B.	
9. SCHUMACHER, K.	9. SCHUMACHER, K.		
15. [BYE]	2. BECKER, B.		
2. BECKER, B.			

But now it all came down to one race and two racers: Xavier Xonora and Jason Chaser.

And they couldn't have been more different.

First there was Xavier who, with his bye in the first round and his two soft victories in the quarters and semis, had raced only 25 laps in the course of the entire day.

Then there was Jason, the very last racer to qualify for the tournament and the driver who had participated in the three most grueling races of the day. During those three races, two of which had gone the full 100-lap distance, he'd racked up an astonishing 290 laps: 2 hours and 20 minutes' worth of racing.

The two cars lined up on the grid.

The *Speed Razor* and the *Argonaut*.

Car No. 1 and Car No. 55.

The crowd fell silent.

Even the sponsors in the VIP tent lowered their champagne to watch.

This was the big one.

The final.

THE FINAL:

XONORA V. CHASER

The final race of the Sponsors' Tournament was nothing short of a match-racing classic.

And for a simple reason: It began with a disaster.

In his superfast Lockheed-Martin, Xavier won the dash from the Start Line and on the first left-hand turn of the race, he cut sharply across Jason's path, clipping the *Argonaut*'s nosewing, snapping it off.

And so, after one lap, Jason pitted and by the time he came out on Lap 2 with a new nosewing, the *Argonaut* was barely a car-length in front of the *Speed Razor*.

The ensuing chase phase was utterly ruthless.

Just as he had done to Horatio Wong earlier in the day, Xavier hounded Jason.

His every turn was perfect. His adherence to the racing line, flawless. It was, quite simply, superb hover car racing, clinical in its precision. He gained a foot on the *Argonaut* with every lap.

But where Wong had failed, Jason didn't falter. He fended Xavier off in the only possible way—by driving equally well, his eyes fixed forward.

And with every lap he survived, the crowd roared ever louder. After the nosewing mishap on the first corner, no one had expected Jason to last more than a few laps. But then, this was the kid who'd survived a 9-lap chase phase earlier in the day.

One lap became five.

The chase phase continued.

Five became eight.

Xavier's chase continued.

Nine laps . . . ten . . . *eleven* . . .

Jason raced grimly, his jaw set.

Xavier pursued him like a bloodhound—lap after perfect lap—at one stage bringing his nosecone to within two inches of the *Argonaut*'s nosewing . . . but not past it.

In the end, Jason held the *Speed Razor* off for an astonishing twelve laps before Xavier was compelled to pit.

Jason never recovered the lost time from that first unexpected pit stop.

The effect was brutal. It meant that as long as they went stop for stop—with him *always* pitting second—he was always going to be one lap behind Xavier, always being chased.

And so the race became one endless chase phase—with Jason always running and Xavier always pursuing him ruthlessly, relentlessly, only ever one mistake away from victory.

Not even pit stops helped. Sally consistently churned out 8-second stops, but Xavier's mech chief, Oliver Koch, was just as good.

20 laps passed—and Jason, exhausted and drained, was driving at the edge of his senses.

40 laps—and Sally wasn't allowed a single mistake in the pits and she didn't make one.

60 laps—and the Bug was starting to get a strained neck from twisting in his seat to check on Xavier behind them.

80 laps—and Xavier just kept on coming.

Kept throwing his perfect laps at Jason, and Jason just kept on going in front of him, equally perfect, like the mechanical rabbit at a greyhound race, forever just out of reach.

And as the race crossed the 90-lap mark, the crowd rose to their feet, many of the students among them saying that if Jason's race against Barnaby had been a grudge match, then this was a death match, a race that was going to go all the way to the 100th lap.

And then on Lap 98 it happened.

Something that no one could have expected.

Both racers pitted: Xavier first, and then Jason, who had to whip all the way around the track before he could dash into the pits for that one last crucial stop.

He shoomed into the pits, and immediately saw that *Xavier was still there*—indeed Oliver Koch was scrambling around the *Speed Razor* like a crazy man while Xavier yelled at him, waving his fists.

And then Jason saw why.

The pressure nozzle on Koch's coolant hose had broken off, and coolant was spraying everywhere. Koch was now frantically attaching a new nozzle to his hose.

Which meant that suddenly, the *Argonaut* and the *Speed Razor* were back on a level playing field again.

Sally worked a killer stop—

—just as Koch got his hose working again—

—with the result being that both cars shot out from their pit bays at almost exactly the same time, only now the *Argonaut*, astonishingly, was slightly ahead of the *Speed Razor*!

The two cars blasted back out onto the track, and with only two laps to run, the *Argonaut* was in the lead!

It was now a one-minute scramble for the Finish Line.

Jason flew.

Xavier charged.

Shoom!-shoom!

One lap to go and Jason still held the lead by half a car-length.

The crowd leaped to their feet.

Last lap.

Jason's eyes never left the track.

Left into the sweeper through the city, blurred buildings swooshing by him on either side . . .

Up and over the crossover . . .

Then into the final right-hander, holding the racing line—and Jason saw the *Speed Razor*'s nosecone enter his left-side peripheral vision, heard the roar of its engines loud in his ears.

The *Speed Razor* was right alongside him! Xavier wasn't giving up.

The two cars took the final turn side by side.

Jason gripped his steering wheel tightly, his knuckles white; clenched his teeth. His bloodshot eyes were wide, on the verge of sensory overload.

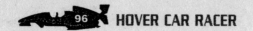

Still the *Speed Razor* kept coming . . . and slowly, gradually, started edging ahead of him!

Jason couldn't believe it. There was nothing he could do! This was the best he could race and still Xavier was going past him.

And with that, the realization hit Jason.

Xavier was too good. Too fast.

This race was slipping out of Jason's grasp.

Xavier was going to win.

And then the home straightaway opened up before them and the *Argonaut* and the *Speed Razor* rushed down it side by side at full throttle, before they shot together through the red laser beam that marked the Finish Line and the winner of the race—of the final—of the day—of the whole entire tournament was—

—Xavier.

By 0.003 of a second. Three *thousandths* of a second.

And as the two cars glided around the track, slowing, Jason sighed with deep relief.

He'd lost. Lost the final—and for that he was bitterly disappointed—but he was also glad that this day, this long day of racing, was finally over.

Almost every member of the 250,000-strong crowd stayed for the winner's ceremony.

They clapped loudly as Xavier stepped triumphantly onto the podium to accept the winner's trophy from

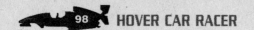

Race Director Calder and Jean-Pierre LeClerq.

Jason could only stand behind the podium, behind the 2nd-place-getter's step, and clap too.

He'd come so far, raced so hard, through four of the most difficult races of his life, and he'd missed out by the smallest fraction of a second.

The applause for Xavier and his team died down, and the announcer's voice came again over the loud-speakers:

"And in second place, Car No. 55, Team Argonaut. Driver: Jason Chaser; Navigator: Bug Chaser; Mech Chief: Sally McDuff."

Head down with disappointment, Jason stepped up onto the podium.

What happened next made him freeze in shock.

The crowd went nuts.

Absolutely, totally *ballistic*.

The colossal roar that they gave him and Sally and the Bug almost brought down the entire stadium.

Flashbulbs popped, horns blared, people raised their

The crowd went nuts.

hands above their heads to clap. Even Xavier was taken aback by the strength of their cheering.

But it was true.

The crowd was giving a bigger cheer to the racer who'd come in *second* than they had for the racer who'd come in first!

Jason was stunned, and at first he didn't understand why this was happening.

Nevertheless, with the Bug and Sally beside him, he took his place on the second tier of the podium and, dressed in his cool new race suit, waved hesitantly to the crowd.

The crowd went even crazier at the gesture, started chanting: "Jason! JASON! *JASON!*"

It was then that Jason saw his mother down in the crowd. She was crying with joy. Beside her, his father, Henry, was busily taking audio-included digital photographs for their family album.

And in that instant Jason began to understand.

Xavier had won the tournament, and won it well, and the crowd respected that.

While for his part Jason had lost—but he had lost well.

After a staggering 390 laps of racing, at the edge of total exhaustion, he had lost by less than a second to a guy who had creamed every other opponent he had faced—and the crowd respected that even *more*.

Jason remembered something his father had once told him: *It's not how we win that defines us, Jason, it's how we lose. Winners come and go, but the racer who goes down fighting will live forever in people's hearts.*

Jason smiled at that as he gazed out over the roaring crowd—the crowd roaring for him.

As he did so, Race Director Calder handed each member of Xavier's winning team an enormous bottle of champagne, and Xavier shook his bottle hard and popped the cork, sending a geyser of champagne shooting into the air above the winner's podium.

That evening, the Chaser family—plus Sally and Scott Syracuse—returned to Chooka's Charcoal Chicken Restaurant for another celebratory dinner.

"Guess what," Sally said as she munched on a burger. "I heard that after the winner's presentation the head of the Lockheed-Martin pro team, Antony Nelson, approached Xavier and asked him if he wanted to apprentice with them at the Italian Run next month."

"No way!" Jason exclaimed. "The Lockheed Factory Team. Wow! To the winner go the spoils, I guess . . ."

"Don't you worry," Henry Chaser said, seeing his disappointment. "Your time'll come. I don't think your efforts today went unnoticed."

"Yeah?" Jason laughed. "Well, I don't see the chiefs of any pro teams walking up to us and offering us a run in a Grand Slam race."

Just as Jason was saying this, a large figure entered the restaurant.

Heads turned, whispers arose—precisely because you don't often see billionaires in takeout chicken joints.

It was Umberto Lombardi.

"Ah-ha!" the big Italian boomed. "Now *this* is my kind of dinner! Three Super Burgers to go, please, madam, with extra cheese! Oh, would anyone else like anything?"

Lombardi sat down beside Martha Chaser. "My sincere apologies, Señora Chaser, for intruding upon your celebrations. But I beg your indulgence, I will not stay for long. I do, however, have a serious question for this wonderful young team."

Everyone at the table fell silent.

Lombardi leaned forward, lowered his voice. "I thought you all raced well today. Very well. No other team out there came close to surviving almost 400 laps of match racing. But you did. More than that. You did that *and you almost won*!

"Now. As you are probably aware, the Italian Run is to be held in three weeks' time. Up until now, my team has only ever run one car in pro events, but lately I've been thinking of expanding the team . . . and adding a second car."

Jason felt a tingle race up his spine. "Yes . . ."

Lombardi went on. "What I was wondering was this: Would the members of Team *Argonaut* like to race the second Lombardi Racing Team car in this year's Italian Run?"

Jason dropped his fork. The Bug blanched. Sally's mouth fell open. Henry Chaser stopped chewing. Martha Chaser's lip started to quiver. Scott Syracuse just kept eating casually.

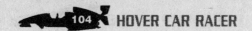

"You . . ." Jason stammered. "You want *us* to race for *you* in the next Grand Slam race?"

"Yes. I do," Lombardi said simply.

Jason swallowed.

This was too much. The enormity of what Lombardi was suggesting rocked through him with the force of an earthquake.

This wouldn't be like any old school race. Or even like the Sponsors' Tournament, for that matter. This would be bigger—much bigger. This would be a professional race against professional racers, in Italy, beamed live to the entire world.

"Well?" Lombardi asked. "Do you race?"

Jason looked at the Bug, who nodded once.

He turned to Sally who, still silent with shock, nodded vigorously.

Then he turned back to Lombardi and said, "You bet we race."

And so it was settled.

Team *Argonaut* was going to Italy.

PART II

THE ITALIAN RUN

THE ITALIAN RUN:
ROME TO VENICE II
(with short cut)

▭	Course
▪▪▪▪▪▪▪▪▪	Pit Crew Route
▪▪▪▪▪▪▪▪	Short cut

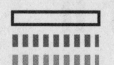

In the hover car racing world, there are four "Grand Slam" races. In order, they are:

The Sydney Classic, held in February.

The London Underground Run, May.

The Italian Run, August.

And the New York Masters, in October.

Naturally, they are all very different kinds of races.

The Sydney race is a typically Australian event—tough and hard and long, a test of endurance, like five-day-long cricket matches or the old Bathurst 1,000-car race. It is a lap race that lasts 20 hours, during which racers do 156 laps of a course that runs past the eight giant ocean-dams that line Australia's eastern coastline, ending underneath the grandest Finish Line in the world: the Sydney Harbour Bridge. Australians call it "the race that stops a nation."

The London Underground Run is a gate race—the most fiendish gate race of all. Held in the subterranean dark of the London subway system, it tests every racer's tactical abilities, seeing how many underground stations they can whip through in 6 hours. No racer has ever "clocked up" every single station.

For its part, the New York Masters is a carnival of racing, four races held over four consecutive days, one race per day—one supersprint, a gate race, one collective pursuit, and finishing it off, an example of the rarest race of all, a long-distance search-and-retrieve "quest" race that takes racers from New York City to Niagara Falls and back again.

The Italian Run, however, has its own unique format.

Held every year in the baking heat of the northern summer, it is a *unidirectional* race. Racers do not do laps around a circuit. Rather, they start in one city and end in another, on the other side of the country.

The race starts in Rome, inside the Colosseum, after which it shoots north, up the spine of Italy, swinging through Florence, Padua, and Milan before it winds up through the Alps and then begins the long trip south down the western coast and between the islands of Sicily and Sardinia. Then it's under the bottom of the boot— where racers can choose to cut the heel if they dare—followed by the final dash up the eastern side of the country to the grand finish in Venice II.

Interestingly, there are *two* pit areas in the Italian Run—one at Leonardo da Vinci International Airport in Fiumicino near Rome and a second directly across the country at Pescara. It is thus the only race in the world where *pit crews* have to travel overland to get to the second stop. It is not unknown for racers to get to Pescara and find that their mech chief has not yet arrived.

Unlike most of the races Jason had run at Race School (which operated under the southern hemisphere rules of racing, such as "car over the line" finishes), the Italian Run operated under the more traditional rules of the northern pro-racing confederations, including a different finishing rule: "driver over the line."

This meant that it was the first racer—driver or navigator, it didn't matter—over the line who won the race, whether *or not* they were in their car. On more than one occasion, a racer, his car broken down or crashed, had *run* (or in Italy, where the Finish Line was over water, swum) over the line to finish the race.

Ultimately, however, the Italian Run is a truly *European* event, and as such it is loved by all of Europe. Every year, millions descend upon Italy for it. Immense crowds line the coastline *of the entire country*, sitting on hills and cliffs and hover grandstands.

For one week in August every year, Italy becomes the center of Europe, buzzing with tourists and race fans—all of them with money to spend. Economists say that the week of the Italian Run injects $60 billion into the Italian economy.

It was into this surging pulsating world that Jason Chaser was about to plunge.

THE INTERNATIONAL RACE SCHOOL
HOBART, TASMANIA

But before Jason and Xavier were to depart for Italy, there were still almost a dozen school races to be run.

While the Race School was very proud to have two of its racers invited to compete in a Grand Slam event, it was made very clear to both Jason and Xavier that while they were away in Italy, the school season would continue without them.

Which meant they had to put as many competition points as possible in the bank before they left. This was less of a problem for Xavier, who was currently leading the School Competition Standings by a clear 30 points.

For Jason, it was tougher. As runner-up in the mid-season tournament, he had garnered a solid 18 points (the tournament being worth double points), lifting him to 7th on the overall Competition Standings. But Italy would take him away from the school competition for eight days, forcing him to miss three whole races. And, Italy aside, he was still mindful that he had to finish the school season in the Top 4 to get an invitation to the New York Masters in October.

He would have to play catch-up when he returned from his adventure in Italy. But heck, he thought, it was worth it—it wasn't every day that a rookie like him got a ride *in a Grand Slam race*.

Dang, he was excited.

Early one morning, a few days after the Sponsors' Tournament, Jason went for a walk by himself out across a grassy headland overlooking Storm Bay. It was a place he went to be alone, to think, and to breathe, away from the frenetic world of racing.

Someone was waiting for him at his spot.

Ariel.

"Hey," Jason walked up beside her.

"Hi there," she said.

Jason hadn't seen her since the day of the tournament, the day he had beaten her, the day after she had—

"You raced well in the tournament, Jason," she said.

"I almost had him. Almost."

"Jason, I couldn't believe you kept up with Xavier for as long as you did. No one could," Ariel said. "And after all those races before. You just never give up."

Jason bowed his head, said nothing.

Ariel said, "You know, I was cheering for you by the end. Sure, after you beat me, I went back to my room for a while and yes, I cried some. But after a while, I switched on the TV and saw that you were still in it, beating everyone. So for the final, I went back out there and sat up in the back of one of the grandstands and watched." She turned to him. "I was proud of you."

"Thanks."

"I also felt I let you down by what I did the night before. With that jerk Fabian."

Someone was waiting for him.

Jason looked at her. "Ariel—"

"No. Don't say anything. I was stupid. I shoulda known better. He told me everything I wanted to hear, but he was only after one thing. Jason, you've been the only person who's been good to me this whole time at Race School. I hope you can forgive me and be my friend again."

Jason was silent for a long time.

Then he said, "You never let me down, Ariel. So we never stopped being friends. Except, of course, out on the track."

And with that Ariel gave him a big hug.

The next twelve races went by in a blur.

Knowing he needed to bank some points before he went to Italy, Jason had solid finishes throughout: four 3rds, three 2nds, and even two wins—although it had to be said that both of his wins came on days when Xavier Xonora decided to take a rest and sit out the race.

This fact actually bothered Jason.

He realized that he had only ever beaten Xavier on one occasion—in Race 25, and even then, it had been in pretty

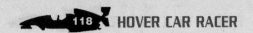

incredible circumstances, after he'd taken the very non-percentage move of skipping his final pit stop.

In any case, his results catapulted Team *Argonaut* up in the Competition Standings and by the time he was leaving for Italy, the Standings looked like this:

THE INTERNATIONAL RACE SCHOOL
CHAMPIONSHIP STANDINGS

AFTER 37 RACES

	DRIVER	NO.	CAR	POINTS
1.	XONORA, X.	1	*Speed Razor*	266
2.	KRISHNA, V.	31	*Calcutta-IV*	235
3.	WASHINGTON, I.	42	*Black Bullet*	224
4.	CHASER, J.	55	*Argonaut*	217
5.	BECKER, B.	09	*Devil's Chariot*	216
6.	WONG, H.	888	*Little Tokyo*	215
7.	SCHUMACHER, K.	25	*Blue Lightning*	213
8.	PIPER, A.	16	*Pied Piper*	212

Xavier was way out in front. A cool 31 points ahead of his nearest rival, he could sit out three more races and still not lose the no. 1 spot.

Jason was in fourth place—but with a bunch of quality racers nipping at his heels. After missing three races, he'd almost certainly drop out of the Top 4.

But that was a battle to be fought another day.

It was time to go to Italy.

The whole of Italy was positively buzzing with excitement when Jason, the Bug, and Sally stepped off Umberto Lombardi's private hover liner at the main wharf of Venice II.

It was as if hover car fever had gripped the entire nation.

Gargantuan images of Alessandro Romba blared out from building-sized hover billboards along the coast—pictures of the world champion holding cola cans or driving sports hover cars.

Multicolored banners fluttered from every lamppost—either in the colors of the Italian flag or of some racing team. People danced in the streets dressed in the uniforms of their favorite teams, sang, drank, and generally had a great time.

The week of the Italian Run was Party Week in Italy. Magazines and newspapers and TV talk shows spoke of only one thing: *La Corsa*. The Race.

Bookmakers did a thriving trade, offering odds on every available result: the winner, the top three finishers *in order*, any-order multiples, or even just a racer finishing in the top five.

The world champ and local hero, Alessandro Romba, was the talk of the town. His victories in Sydney and London had every race fan wondering if he might be the first racer ever to complete the Golden Grand Slam— winning all four Grand Slam races in one year. Indeed, he had not even been cleanly *passed* in a Grand Slam race this year. He appeared on the talk shows and every Italian loved him like a son.

The French racer, Fabian, was also doing the media rounds. On one occasion, Jason saw him being interviewed on a racing show:

The interviewer was asking Fabian about what he had seen at the Race School in Australia.

"There is a lot of talent down there," Fabian said. "A lot of talent. And the two students who have come here are two of the best young drivers there."

"And what about the female driver at the Race School?" the interviewer asked. "Much fuss was made over her enrollment. What did you make of her?"

Fabian's eyes glinted meanly.

"She was, quite frankly, a nonevent. She was defeated in the first round of the tournament, quite decisively. Call me a dinosaur, but I personally see no place for women in hover car racing."

Jason had scowled at the TV.

But then to his surprise the eyes of the media—always hungry, always looking for new fodder—soon fell on the two young racers who would be making their Grand Slam debuts in the Italian Run: Xavier Xonora and him.

Xavier seemed to take the media attention in stride. Perhaps it was his experience as a royal figure. Perhaps it was the slick public relations machine of the Lockheed-

Martin Factory Team selecting the right talk shows for him to go on. Perhaps, Jason thought, Xavier was just made to be a superstar.

The media (especially the society pages) portrayed Xavier as the dutiful protégé, the sharp-eyed student who would be watching and learning from the master, his No. 1 in the Lockheed-Martin Team, Alessandro Romba. His goals were modest—"I'd just love a top ten finish"—and within a few days he was being hailed as the heir apparent to Romba as the heartthrob of international racing.

Jason had a tougher time of it—just seeing himself portrayed on TV, on magazine covers, in the papers was scary enough.

The media had latched onto his youth. Even though he would be fifteen on Wednesday, he was portrayed as a brilliant young upstart, the fourteen-year-old *wunderkind*—but despite that, still ultimately a boy venturing into a man's world.

He was a curiosity, an oddity—like the bearded lady at the circus—and he didn't like being viewed that way.

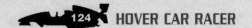

At the first news story that claimed he was out of his depth, he wanted to write a letter to the editor. After the twentieth one, he just fumed silently.

He wished Scott Syracuse were there, but his teacher had stayed back at the Race School—he did, after all, have other students to watch over in their school races. Syracuse had said he would try to get to Italy for the race on Sunday.

Jason hoped he would make it.

Although the Italian Run actually began in Rome, Team *Argonaut* was based in Venice II, since the entire canal city belonged to Umberto Lombardi.

Jason was staying at the Lombardi Grand Hotel, in a suite that turned out to be the third-best apartment in all of Venice II. The best one, of course, belonged to Lombardi himself. The second-best went to Team Lombardi's no. 1 driver, Pablo Riviera.

In any case, Jason's apartment was bigger than most of the houses he knew. Wide and modern, with ultra-expensive hover furniture, it featured panoramic views of both the

Adriatic Sea and Venice II's astonishing recreation of St. Mark's Square.

The week stretched out before him:

Today was Monday.

The official Pole Position Shootout session would be held on Friday, on a tight mini-course up the spine of central Italy. That would be followed by a gala dinner on Friday night.

The Italian Run itself would be held on Sunday.

For most racers, this lead-up week would be filled with practice sessions on the course itself, some sponsors' events, and a few invitation-only galas put on by individual teams.

Importantly for Jason, the lead-up week gave him time to meet the members of the Lombardi Racing Team. For while he would be racing with his regular team—the Bug and Sally—they would be supported by a fully equipped engineering and technical team from Lombardi, known as "E&T."

Most significantly of all—and a little sadly for Jason—

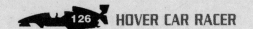

this would be the first time that he would *not* race in the *Argonaut*.

No, in this race he would be flying in a brand-new Ferrari F-3000 emblazoned in the Lombardi Team colors of black with yellow slashes.

Compared to the little *Argonaut*, the Ferrari F-3000 was a beast of a machine: bigger, faster, and meaner. A far newer Ferrari, it had roughly the same bulletlike shape as the *Argonaut*, only it was sleeker, more streamlined.

Once Jason had dreamed of driving an F-3000, but now that he was here, he kind of wished he'd be racing in the *Argonaut*.

But he shook the thought away as he gazed at the chunky F-3000.

He and his team had four days to tame this beast.

For the first two days of Race Week—Monday and Tuesday—Jason practiced in his new F-3000 under the intense glare of media hover copters and the paparazzi's telephoto lenses. A crush of journalists was always waiting

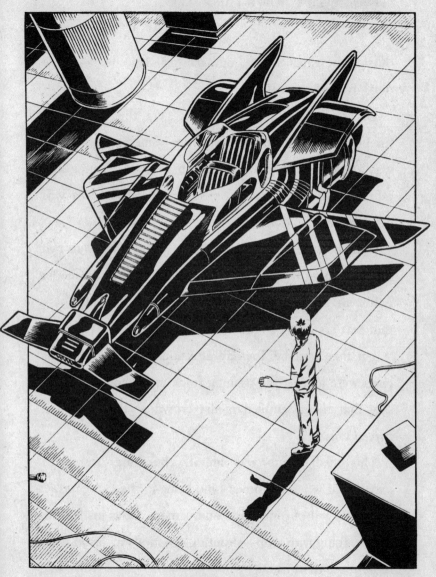

A beast of a machine

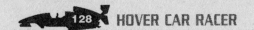

outside the gates of the Lombardi training course on the outskirts of Venice II.

On the Tuesday, he met Pablo Riviera, the no. 1 driver for Lombardi Racing and liked him immediately. Riviera was a twenty-six-year-old Colombian driver. Young and talented but not quite a top-tier racer yet, Riviera was generous in his advice:

"The best tip I can give you," he said, "is to go to bed early. Training will weary you, but dealing with the media will wear you out entirely. Trust me. And the only thing that matters is to be ready on race day."

But then, on the Tuesday afternoon, as Jason and his team were leaving the training track in his hover-limo, he saw that the assembled media crowd at the gates had *tripled* in size.

This media mob was literally bubbling over with excitement when the hover-limo came to the exit gates.

The crowd of journalists and camera crews jostled the car—forcing it to stop—shouting questions at Jason with more force than usual.

And then, beyond them, he saw the reason.

There, grinning like the Cheshire Cat, stood the French driver, Fabian.

Jason and the others stepped out of the limo.

"*Jason!*" the reporters yelled. "*Jason!* Over here!"

"Jason! How do you respond to Fabian's invitation!"

Jason frowned. "Invitation? What invitation?"

Fabian stepped forward theatrically, his French accent oily-smooth. "Ladies and gentlemen. Ladies and gentlemen. Please! Leave young Jason alone. This is all very new to him."

The crowd of hacks took a collective step back and fell silent.

"Jason," Fabian said with more familiarity than Jason liked, "my personal sponsor, the Circus Maximus Beer Company, has decided to stage an exhibition race tomorrow at sunset, in their newly built Circus Maximus. It is to be a one-on-one match race between me and an opponent of my choosing. We are calling it Fabian's Challenge . . ."

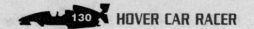

The media crowd was hanging on Fabian's every word and Fabian knew it.

He went on innocently: "I just happened to mention on television this afternoon that I would love to race against the determined young driver everyone is talking about. You. What do you say, Jason? Do you want to race?"

Every microphone in the media throng swung to Jason's lips.

And in that instant, the world froze for Jason.

Later, he wouldn't even remember the words coming out of his mouth—but he heard them quite clearly as he saw himself on every news channel on TV later that afternoon.

"You're on," he'd answered to Fabian's challenge.

The rest of that afternoon and evening was spent talking on the phones with Lombardi and his E&T technicians.

Far from being angry at Jason's acceptance of the challenge, Lombardi *loved* the idea of one of his drivers participating in an exhibition race against Fabian.

"Jason! I may be rich, but my team—in the broader scheme of the racing world—is a midlevel team. Pablo is good, but he too is midrange. Certainly not good enough to attract the attention of someone like Fabian. But you! Yes! Lord, think of the publicity such a race will bring!"

But his enthusiasm only went so far.

He didn't want to endanger a new Ferrari F-3000 in an exhibition race. Which was why he allowed his team of engineers to put a brand-new set of Ferrari XP-7 magneto drives and a super-aerodynamic F-3000 tailfin on the *Argonaut*, to bring it up to speed with Fabian's Renault.

The phones didn't stop ringing all evening.

People were running every which way in Jason's apartment.

And in the middle of it all, Jason went into his room and made a single phone call himself.

██

THE CIRCUS MAXIMUS
ROME, ITALY (WEDNESDAY OF RACE WEEK)

Illuminated by the diffused orange glow of the setting Italian sun, the stadium looked exactly like the famous Roman chariot-racing arena—a gigantic oval-shaped racetrack, flanked on the outer circumference by mammoth grandstands; all of it built in a faux-Roman style on a stretch of flat reclaimed land on the western coast of Italy, not far from Rome.

The only difference between this and the Circus Maximus of old was the scale.

Each of its two straightaways was eight miles long—so that it would take the average hover car roughly two minutes to complete each lap, one minute for each straightaway.

Red neon signs for the CIRCUS MAXIMUS BEER CO. blazed out from the upper flanks of the stadium.

Before a cheering, heaving, thriving crowd of 2 million spectators—all of them fueled on free beer—two tiny hover cars lined up on the grid.

Fabian's purple and gold Renault Tricolore-VII, known as the *Marseilles Falcon*.

And beside it: the *Argonaut*, looking resplendent in spanking-new coats of white, silver, and blue paint. Plus one new feature: its new tailfin was now painted in Lombardi black and yellow.

Just before the race, Jason and Fabian posed for photos on the track—the modern-day charioteers standing beside their chariots, holding their helmets, flanked by bikini-clad girls and beer company executives, in front of the baying crowd.

By the look on his face, Fabian was clearly pleased by the extra attention the young Chaser boy was bringing to his exhibition event. That today, August 6, also happened to be Jason's fifteenth birthday was a bonus—the media had painted Fabian as a man giving a boy the most incredible birthday opportunity ever.

For his part, as he stood beside Fabian, smiling for the cameras, Jason eyed the *Marseilles Falcon* and its notorious nosewing.

Fabian's car featured a controversial "bladed" nosewing. Two vertical fins jutted upward from its outer tips, their forward edges as sharp as knives, hence the term "bladed." Renault claimed the sharpness was simply aerodynamic. Other racers claimed Fabian used his bladed fins to damage their cars in the rough and tumble of racing. For the moment, the fins were allowed by the governing body of racing, the International Hover Car Racing Association. But every racer knew—stay away from them.

The photo session ended, and Fabian jumped into his car.

Jason, however, dashed to his pit bay, to the toilet there—an act that made everybody in the grandstands laugh. The rookie, it seemed, was nervous.

He emerged moments later, strapping his helmet in place. He stepped into the *Argonaut*, joining the Bug, ready to race.

The exhibition race was an absolute beauty.

As the *Marseilles Falcon* and the *Argonaut* shot down the first straightaway, the delighted crowd did a Mexican Wave alongside them.

The race was twenty laps and at first Fabian took the lead—at times doing playful trick moves to please the crowd.

Jason trailed him doggedly, showing his trademark determination, and during one of Fabian's playful moments, he ducked inside him and passed him.

Obviously surprised, Fabian gave chase and, after a lap, retook the lead.

But it was to be the first of many lead changes, with Jason entering into the spirit of things—to everyone's surprise, he also performed some daring aerobatics whenever he took the lead: flat lateral skids or the odd corkscrew roll.

The crowd cheered with delight.

But then the race neared its final stages, and the tricks ceased, and when the *Argonaut* slipped inside the *Marseilles Falcon* on the second-to-last turn, it became a flat-out—and deadly serious—dash for the Finish Line.

Down the back straightaway.

Twin bullets.

Into the final 180-degree turn—the *Argonaut* taking the standard apex, Fabian starting wide and scything inside with the precision of a surgeon, the *Falcon*'s deadly bladed nosewing coming within inches of the *Argonaut*'s own nose—and the two cars ended up side by side as they shot down the main straightaway, kicking up identical yellow sandclouds behind them, before hitting the line together . . .

THE CIRCUS MAXIMUS
ROME, ITALY (WEDNESDAY OF RACE WEEK)

The roar of the crowd said it all. They knew who had won. The rookie, Chaser, had got it by half a car-length.

Jason's fist shot into the air as he cruised around the track, waving to the crowd.

Fabian's car came alongside the *Argonaut*, and Fabian offered Jason the "racer's salute": a short touch of the helmet with his right hand. It was like shaking hands after a tennis match—you always did it after a match race.

Jason returned the salute.

The two cars completed a full circuit to a standing ovation, before coming to a halt in the main straight, in front of the VIP box.

Fabian stepped out of his car and shook his head in mock disbelief, as if to say: "Can you believe that? How about this young guy?"

He went over to the *Argonaut* just as Jason and the Bug lifted themselves out of the cockpit. Fabian went to shake Jason's hand, but Jason's gloved hands instead went to his own helmet. He took it off—

—to reveal that the pilot of the *Argonaut*, the racer who had just beaten Fabian in a wonderfully entertaining match race, wasn't Jason Chaser at all.

Standing there in the middle of the Circus Maximus, wearing Jason Chaser's racing leathers, holding Jason Chaser's helmet, and standing beside Jason Chaser's pint-sized navigator, stood Ariel Piper.

Live on international television, Fabian's jaw hit the dusty ground.

"But . . ." he stammered. "We had our photo taken before the—"

"Looks like the Jason Chaser who went to the men's room just before the race wasn't the Jason Chaser who came out," Ariel said. "Now, Fabian. What was it you were saying about women and hover car racing?"

The crowd was stunned—at first.

Then they roared their hilarious approval.

Ariel could only smile with immense satisfaction.

And far away to the north, at the empty Lombardi practice track, without a journalist, photographer, or hover copter in sight, Jason Chaser stepped into his Ferrari F-3000 and practiced—practiced, practiced, practiced—in glorious peace and quiet.

The best birthday present ever.

Ariel could only smile.

THE POLE POSITION SHOOTOUT
ROME, ITALY (FRIDAY OF RACE WEEK)

Jason's black and yellow Ferrari F-3000 banked at almost right angles as it blasted in a wide arc around the Colosseum.

Then it executed a quick series of zigzags through the streets of Rome, before it swung out into the open countryside, onto the final section of the Pole Position Shootout course—a fiendish stretch of track known as the Chute.

This winding S-shaped section of track was actually a long narrow trench dug into the earth, spanned by a multitude of sponsor-bridges.

The key feature of the Chute were the four barriers

spaced out along its length. Built into each barrier was an ultranarrow gateway—so narrow that a hover car could only pass through each opening *on its side*. That the gateways were positioned alternately on the far left and right sides of each barrier made it a brutal driving challenge.

It was hard enough racing through the Chute alone during the Pole Position Shootout—in the Italian Run itself, there were several Chute sections and you had to negotiate them *with other racers buzzing all around you*.

In any case, the Pole Position Shootout was a time trial—with the fastest driver through the Shootout Course starting Sunday's race in pole position—so racers entered the Shootout Course one at a time.

Each was allowed three runs over the course, and their best time counted.

That Friday morning, one after the other, each racer entered the Shootout Course.

This was Jason's third run and as he hit the Chute he was flying like a rocket. His previous times that day hadn't been spectacular—but this run was *fast*.

The walls of the trench rushed by him at astronomical speed, bending left and right and then—*whoosh!*—he tilted his F-3000 sideways and shot through the first gateway.

Three more banking maneuvers later, he shot through the final gateway to the roars of the crowd. His eyes flashed to the electronic scoreboard:

THE ITALIAN RUN

POLE POSITION SHOOTOUT

DRIVER	NO.	TEAM	TIME
1. ROMBA, A.	1	*Lockheed-Martin*	0:50.005
2. FABIAN	17	*Renault*	0:50.230
3. LEWICKI, D.	23	*USAF Racing*	0:51.015
4. CARVER, A.	24	*USAF Racing*	0:51.420
5. HASSAN, R.	2	*Lockheed-Martin*	0:51.995
6. MARTINEZ, C.	44	*Boeing-Ford*	0:52.110

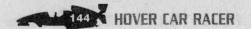

7.	IDEKI, K.	11	*Yamaha Racing*	0:52.525
8.	TROUVEAU, E.	40	*Renault*	0:52.740
9.	XONORA, X.	3	*Lockheed-Martin*	0:53.300
10.	RIVIERA, P.	12	*Lombardi Racing*	0:53.755
11.	PETERS, B.	05	*General Motors*	0:54.300
12.	CHASER, J.	55	*Lombardi Racing*	0:54.841

12th.

12th was good. Jason certainly hadn't expected to win pole. He was just hoping to put in a good performance—and come out of the Chute with his car in one piece. Hell, if he'd managed a place in the top ten, he'd have been over the moon.

But 12th out of a total of 28 starters made him pretty happy.

"Not bad," Sally said. "Not bad at all . . . for a first timer."

She messed up Jason's hair. "Nice racing, Superstar."

That evening, even though he really didn't want to go, Jason was obliged to attend the official Gala Dinner for the Italian Run.

If the gala for the Sponsors' Tournament at the Race School had been opulent, then this dinner was in another league altogether.

It was held in the Piazza de Campidoglio—the famous triple-palace plaza designed by Michelangelo situated on the Capitoline Hill—and in the blazing glare of spotlights pointed up into the sky, the glittering piazza looked like something out of a fairy tale.

Hover limousines unloaded the cream of Europe's rich and famous—billionaires, movie stars, rock singers, and of course, racers. Gushing reporters breathlessly announced each new arrival on the red carpet.

For Jason, though, it was just another dinner.

"How long do we have to stay?" he asked Sally as they walked through the crush of black tie–wearing guests, searching for their table, the Bug staying close behind them.

"Lombardi says we only have to stay until the speeches," Sally said. "Then we're free to leave."

"Thank God. Any sign of Mr. Syracuse? Is he still coming?"

Sally said, "Last time I spoke with him, he was hoping to get here on Saturday. They had a race on at the school today—you know, the one Ariel had to go back for—and he had to stay for that."

"Any idea who won—" Jason said as he slid past a tight cluster of people and abruptly bumped into someone he knew.

Xavier Xonora.

An awkward moment.

Jason, Sally, and the Bug faced their rival, the Black Prince.

"Hello, Xavier," Jason said.

"Chaser."

"Thought you drove well in the Shootout today," Jason said. "Tough competition here. Where'd you end up? 9th?"

"That's correct. 9th. But then my goal *was* to finish in the top ten, so all in all, I'm pleased."

At that moment, Xavier's father, King Francis of Monesi, came up behind Xavier. "Excuse me, son. I have someone—" at which point the King saw Jason and his team and he cut himself off. "Oh."

"Hey there, your Highness," Jason said good-naturedly. "Good to see you again."

The king seemed taken aback, as if he didn't expect Jason to be capable of speech, let alone friendly speech. "It's, er, nice to see you again, too, Master Chaser. Xavier? I have someone I'd like you to meet. When you're finished talking with Master Chaser." The king nodded to Jason. "Have a . . . pleasant evening."

When his father had left, Xavier turned to Jason, ice in his glare. "So. Chaser. Are your parents here? I hear there are some very good trailer parks on the outskirts of Rome."

"You know, Xavier, you're a great racer. It's a shame you're such a *jerk*."

And with that, Jason went to his table.

Beside his meeting with Xavier, Jason had two other interesting encounters at the gala dinner.

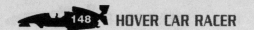

The first came midway through the main course, when he went to the rest room.

As he washed his hands at the basin, a short, weedy-looking Indian man came alongside him, also washing his hands. Without even looking at him, the Indian man said, "Ooh-ooh, my oh my. Look who it is. It's Jason Chaser, hover car racer. How are you feeling, Jason?"

Jason turned. "Do I know you?"

The Indian fellow extended his hand. "Ooh. Pardon me, pardon me. How rude of me. Gupta is my name. Ravi Narendra Gupta."

"Again: do I know you?"

"No, but I know you, Jason."

Jason said, "Are you involved in one of the racing teams?"

Ravi Gupta smiled in a way that Jason immediately disliked. "Ooh, sort of yes. Sort of no. I'm just a very *interested* observer of racing."

Jason became guarded. "You're not a reporter, are you?"

"Ooh, no. No no no! Certainly not! I promise you, young

Jason, I am no reporter. Just an interested observer. For instance, I'm keen to know how you're finding top level racing. You seemed to manage the shootout very well today."

"I was pleased to finish mid-field."

"How do you like the F-3000? Not too much grunt for you?"

"It's a good car." Jason didn't understand why Gupta was asking him this.

Just then, Umberto Lombardi entered the men's room—and before Jason knew what had happened, Gupta had vanished, gone in an instant.

Lombardi saw the perplexed look on Jason's face. "Something wrong, my young star?"

Jason looked all around. The Indian was indeed nowhere to be seen. "No . . . no . . . nothing's wrong."

Jason's second interesting encounter of the evening occurred immediately after the speeches had ended.

Just as the applause for the president of Italy was dying down and Jason was preparing to leave the dinner and go

A short, weedy-looking Indian man came alongside him.

home, an absolutely beautiful young girl suddenly sat down next to him.

"Hi!" she said. "You're Jason Chaser, aren't you?"

"Er . . . uh . . . yeah," Jason stammered, awestruck.

She was about his age, fifteen, with big blue eyes and dazzling blond hair. She wore an expensive sky-blue cocktail dress that just shone with style. In short, she was the prettiest girl Jason had ever seen in his life.

"I'm Dido," she said in an Italian–American accent. "Dido Emanuele, and I'm a *huge* fan. I watched you on TV in that school tournament a few weeks ago and then I saw you in the shootout today. You're *amazing*, and look at you, you're so young! Okay, that was dumb. Sorry, I don't mean to sound so pathetic, like some starstruck groupie. I just saw you sitting over here and decided I had to say hi. So . . . *hi*!"

Jason was speechless before her. "Th . . . thanks."

"Well," Dido said. "You look like you're getting ready to go. I won't bother you any more. Maybe—hopefully—I'll see you around."

And with that, she stood and flashed her big blue eyes at him, and Jason melted.

Dido skipped happily away from the table. Jason just watched her go.

Sally McDuff broke the spell by clapping him on the shoulder. "Nice work, Romeo. I didn't know you were such a sweet-talker with the ladies. Let's analyze your performance during that conversation: 'Er . . . uh . . . yeah,' and 'Th . . . thanks.' Heads up, Champ, I'm sure you'll do better next time. Come on, let's go home and get you to bed. Tomorrow, we rest. Then on Sunday, we race."

THE LOMBARDI GRAND HOTEL
VENICE II, ITALY (SATURDAY)

Saturday was a "focus" day for Jason.

A time to sit and contemplate and focus on the big race ahead.

With the press camped outside his hotel, Jason stayed in his suite for most of the day, mainly staring out the window at the sea.

The Bug played headset car-racing computer games, his form of relaxation. Sally paced a lot, and read and reread her Pro Circuit Pit Bay Rules and Regulations Manual.

In the afternoon, Henry and Martha Chaser arrived in Venice II. They would have come earlier in the week, but Henry had had to work on the farm. Now, they just hung out nearby—Henry marveling at the suite ("Gosh, it's so big"), Martha knitting as usual.

Midway through the day, Jason's racing leathers arrived: a brand-new black flight suit with yellow piping down the arms and legs, and LOMBARDI RACING splashed across the chest. Yellow gloves, black boots, and a sleek yellow helmet completed the package. The Bug and Sally received similar outfits.

And then in the early evening, Jason made a fateful decision. Tired of room service, he went down to the hotel's executive dining room for some dinner.

The executive dining room was an exclusive restaurant reserved for those guests staying in the upper floors of the hotel.

As he sat down on his own, Jason saw Dido sitting at another table with two adults, presumably her parents.

"Dido . . . ?" he said.

"Jason!" Dido came over.

"I didn't know you were staying here."

"Yeah, I am, well, thanks to my parents," Dido said.

"They're, well, kinda rich. Listen, you look like you want to be alone, to prepare for the race, so I'll just leave you be—"

"No," Jason blurted. "It's okay. You don't have to go. I mean, if you . . . if you wanted and if . . . if it was okay with your folks . . . maybe you'd like to have dinner with me."

A wonderful smile sprang across Dido's face. "I'd like that. Let me go and ask."

Moments later, Jason was seated by a huge bay window overlooking the Grand Canal, dining with the beautiful Dido Emanuele by the light of a lone candle—two teenagers looking like a pair of adults, dining in one of the most exclusive restaurants in the world.

They talked into the evening, and Jason loved every minute of it. Dido was smart, funny, captivating, and *normal*. And better still, she seemed to like him too! Before he knew it, the restaurant was empty and they were sitting there all alone, and it was only when Sally McDuff appeared at his side that he came out of his trancelike state.

"Well, hey there, Superstar," Sally said. "We were all

wondering where you'd got to. Thought you might have taken an introspective stroll or something. But then it got a bit late for that. It's almost midnight, you know."

"It's *what*?" Jason looked at his watch. She was right. It was 11:55. "Dido, I'm sorry. I have to go. I've got to get some sleep. Big day tomorrow."

"Hey, no problem at all," Dido said. "I'm sorry for keeping you this long. I didn't even notice the time. Thank you for dinner."

Jason nodded. "No. Thank *you*. I really enjoyed it."

He left with Sally.

Sally watched him as they walked, bemused. He looked like he was walking on air.

She shook her head. "You know, that's what I like about you, Jason. You're a quick learner. Yesterday, you were a stammering idiot in front of that girl. Today you're as smooth as Casanova himself. Nice work, kiddo. Nice work. Now get some sleep. Tomorrow's going to be a big day."

The beautiful Dido Emanuele

THE ITALIAN RUN
ROME, ITALY (SUNDAY, RACE DAY)

"Racers. This is your three-minute warning. Would all pit personnel please vacate the start area," intoned a stern voice over the public address system.

The starting area for the Italian Run was the Colosseum. Every racer started from the same spot, in the exact center of the 2000-year-old Roman amphitheater.

The pole sitter took off first, blasting out of the stadium, followed by the second-place starter who, sitting on a car-sized conveyor belt, would be cranked out onto the starting grid, ready to go exactly twenty seconds later. Then would come the third car, and the fourth, and so on, all drawn out into the arena on the conveyor belt, a new racer starting every twenty seconds until all twenty-eight had commenced the race.

In the dark stone conveyor-belt tunnel, Jason and the Bug stood a short distance away from their F-3000—now christened the *Argonaut II*—12th in line on the belt.

Jason's eyes scanned the preparation chamber.

"He's not coming," he said.

Sally had a headset phone strapped to her head. "He's not answering his phone either."

There was no sign of Scott Syracuse. He hadn't arrived in Italy yesterday, nor had he left any messages for Jason and the team. No "Good luck," no anything.

Having his parents here was one thing, but Jason had hoped Syracuse would come—if only to give him some professional words of support.

"*Racers. This is your one-minute warning. Pole sitter to the starting grid, please.*"

"Jason . . ." Sally pressed him toward the *Argonaut II*.

But Jason was still scanning the area for Syracuse.

The simple truth was, he was nervous as anything.

THE ITALIAN RUN:
ROME TO VENICE II
(with short cut)

▭	Course
▪▪▪▪▪▪▪▪▪	Pit Crew Route
▪▪▪▪▪▪▪▪▪	Short cut

ITALY

Venice II

Sardinia   Rome

Sicily

In fact, he'd never felt this nervous before in his life. His stomach was positively churning. He couldn't believe this: *He was about to race in a pro event.* You could watch pro races on TV every weekend, but until you were in one, you never knew what it was really like.

Then, finally, he turned to face his car—and glimpsed a flash of movement near the tailfin of the *Argonaut II*. For an instant, he could have sworn that he'd seen someone lurking there—someone small—a man he had met before.

Ravi Gupta.

Jason went to investigate, but found no one near the *Argonaut II*'s tail. He scanned the tailfin itself but found nothing out of place or out of order.

And then—lo and behold—he saw Gupta, standing a short distance away, over with another driver.

Gupta caught him looking and waved back happily.

Jason eyed him carefully: "Sally, do you know that guy? The guy waving at me."

"Yeah, of course," Sally's voice became a low growl.

"He's Ravi Gupta, and you don't want to get caught up with him. He's bad news."

"What's he do?" Jason remembered the weird questions Gupta had asked him on Friday night: how he was coping with top-level racing; how he was finding the F-3000's extra power.

Sally said, "You don't know who Ravi Gupta is? Sorry, kiddo, but sometimes I forget you're still so young. Ravi Gupta is a gambler. A bookmaker. Heck, one of the biggest bookmakers in the racing world. Now, come on." Sally handed him his helmet. "You got other things to worry about."

"Right," Jason took the helmet.

Then he and the Bug climbed into the two-man cockpit and strapped themselves in.

Once they were settled, Jason exhaled. "Hoo-ah."

The Bug said something in his earpiece.

"Yeah, me too," Jason replied. "Mine's churning like a clothes dryer."

• • •

With a dramatic mechanical clanking, the giant conveyor belt rumbled to life and the supersleek, silver and black Lockheed-Martin of Alessandro Romba, the pole sitter and current world champion, was drawn out into the main arena of the Colosseum . . .

. . . and the 60,000-strong VIP crowd packed into the ancient amphitheater roared as one.

Romba's car, *La Bomba*, came to a halt, now pointed like a missile toward the external archway of the Colosseum. The exit to the course itself.

"*Twenty seconds to race-start . . .*" came the voice. "*Would the second-place racer please stand by . . .*"

A 20-second digital countdown ticked downward on a giant scoreboard, beeping with every second . . .

. . . the crowd leaned forward . . .

. . . *beep-beep-beep* . . .

. . . Jason watched Romba's car from the stone tunnel, his heart in his throat.

Sally patted his shoulder. "Good luck, my boys. I'll be waiting for you at both pit stops."

"Thanks, Sally. Have a good race."

Beep-beep-beep . . .

Then the countdown hit zero and a shrill beep screamed and the lights went green and Alessandro Romba screamed off the starting grid, blasting out of the Colosseum and the Italian Run was underway.

As soon as Romba was out of the stadium, the conveyor-belt tunnel erupted with activity.

The great belt immediately rumbled into action once again.

"*Twenty seconds to next racer. Second-placed racer to the grid . . .*"

The 20-second countdown restarted and the second-placed car—Fabian's purple and gold Renault—was drawn out of the prep tunnel and into the sunlight, and Jason heard the roar of the crowd.

The conveyor-belt line of racers shunted forward one place, all of them watching tensely as they awaited their turn to move out onto the starting grid and into the glare of the hysterical crowd.

The countdown hit zero and Fabian shot off the mark.

"*Twenty seconds to next racer. Third-placed racer to the grid . . .*"

Jason watched each car shunt along the conveyor belt, take its place on the grid, and shoot out of sight—they looked like bullets being loaded into the chamber of a gun and then fired.

His nerves got tighter and tighter with every passing moment. Watching each car go was almost hypnotic— shunt-shunt, *beep-beep*, blast off; shunt-shunt, *beep-beep*, blast off . . .

And then, surprising him, the announcer said: "*Twenty seconds to next racer. Twelfth-placed racer, to the grid . . .*"

He'd become so preoccupied with the rhythm of each new car moving out onto the grid and blasting off that it surprised him when his turn came around.

And so Jason sat in the *Argonaut II* as it was drawn out of the tunnel and into the dazzling sunlight—

—where it entered another world.

The crowd packed into the ancient stadium howled and roared, clapped and screamed. They were absolutely *wild*. And these were the VIPs. Jason couldn't imagine what the ordinary race fans out on the course would be like.

The *Argonaut II* jolted to a halt on the starting grid.

Locked and loaded.

The arched exit tunnel leading out of the Colosseum yawned before Jason.

The Bug whispered something.

"You can say that again, little brother," Jason replied. "Hang on."

The digital countdown hit zero, the lights went green, and Jason floored it. His Ferrari F-3000 exploded out of the Colosseum and he began his first Grand Slam race.

His Ferrari F-3000 exploded out of the Colosseum.

Speed.

Supercharged, blinding speed.

Rome whistled past Jason's cockpit in a hyperfast blur of horizontal streaks—before he abruptly left the city in his wake and shot up the spine of Italy, knifing up the Autostrata, heading toward Florence.

The entire freeway was lined with spectactors three-hundred deep.

Ahead of him, he could make out the tailfins of the two cars that had started immediately before him. Twenty seconds wasn't much of a head start and they were already dueling.

And then—*bam!*—Jason swung into the first Chute section

of the course and suddenly he was right on the tails of the two racers ahead of him. They'd both had to slow down at a gateway when neither would give way and now Jason was on their tails—trying to gauge whether or not he could pass them before the next narrow aperture.

And that was the thing: multiple cars in a Chute was little more than a high-speed game of "Chicken"—a who-dares-wins race to each aperture—all played out at a deadly 440 mph.

Jason waited for his moment, for his chance to make his move when suddenly—*shoom!*—he was himself overtaken by the car that had started *behind* him, in 13th place.

The car—a member of the Boeing-Ford factory team—had screamed by so close that it actually scratched a chunk of paint off Jason's right wingtip.

"Dang it! Never saw him!" Jason yelled.

"*Make a note, kiddo. We ain't in Kansas anymore,*" Sally's voice said in his earpiece.

And then suddenly, Jason was out of the chute section and he beheld Florence ahead of him, its famous terra-cotta dome rising above a low cityscape in the center of a wide hazy valley. Every roof on every hill was covered with spectators.

Jason ripped down the Arno River, swooping under its famous bridges. As he swept under the Ponte Vecchio, Jason went left, around a bridge pylon, while the Boeing-Ford that had got him in the Chute went right, and as they came out on the other side, Jason was in front and the crowd on the bridge cheered.

The race shot northward, through Padua—coming tantalizingly close to the ultimate finish of the race, Venice II—and the monumental crowds there.

Giant hover grandstands, floating above the hills, pivoted in midair to watch the cars go by, before turning back around, ready to catch them when they would come through in about two hours' time at the business end of the race.

Then it was into Milan—the cars banking round the great Sforza Castle, before heading into the most treacherous part of the race: the vertiginous cliff-edged roads and tunnels of the Alps.

• • •

As always happened in the Italian Run, the field bunched up on the tight twisting roads of the Alps—and here the top racers made their moves.

Showing exceptional skill, Xavier climbed two places, to 7th, whipping past Etienne Trouveau of the Renault team and Kamiko Ideki, the notoriously unpredictable Japanese driver for the Yamaha team, known to fans everywhere as "Kamikaze" Ideki.

Back in 12th, Jason also moved up the field, first taking the Australian driver, Brock Peters, before sweeping past his own teammate for the Lombardi team, Pablo Riviera, in a daring round-the-outside maneuver.

Up to 10th . . .

And then the first crash of the race occurred and it caused a sensation—because it was the 3rd-placed driver, Dwayne Lewicki of the U.S. Air Force Team, who'd bowed out. Lewicki had thundered at 280 mph into the arched entryway of a tunnel as he'd tried to pass the 2nd-placed Fabian.

Lewicki had tried to duck inside Fabian, but the Frenchman wasn't having any of it, and he'd held his line as he'd entered the tunnel, cutting across the bow of Lewicki's fighter jet–shaped car—the razor-sharp blades of Fabian's nosewing *shearing the left wing of Lewicki's nosewing clean off*, causing Lewicki to lose control and slam into the archway.

Everyone moved up a place.

Romba was out in front.

Fabian, 2nd.

Xavier, 6th.

Jason: 9th.

In the top ten . . .

Down through the mountains, sweeping through Milan again, then into the third Chute section of the course between Milan and the French border, before making a tight hairpin at the glorious white-walled city of Nice.

And then the racers hit the coastline.

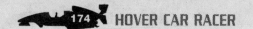

This was the most spectacular section of the course—with every single mile of the Italian coast teeming with crowds.

One after the other, the lead cars shot down the coastal straightaway, shooting through faux-Roman archways that rose up out of the sea a hundred or so yards out from the shoreline. The archways were in a staggered formation—forcing the racers to sweep down the coast in broad S-shaped swoops rather than in a continuous straight line, the whole section—like all the other "ocean" sections of the course—flanked by red demagnetizing lights.

As the ocean swept by under his nosewing, Jason saw on his dials that his mags were way down on magnetic power by now, severely worn by the tight traverse through the mountains and the three Chute sections.

But that was normal—they were coming up on the pit section at Fiumicino Airport outside Rome, and everyone would be pitting there.

The *Argonaut II* screamed down the coast at almost full speed, 510 mph, ever-closing on the hover car in front of it: car no. 40, the *Vizir*, the second car of the Renault team, driven by Etienne Trouveau.

Jason saw Trouveau's tailfin, saw it wobble slightly after whipping through an archway, losing the "line" needed to take the next Roman archway properly.

So Jason seized the opportunity, gunned the *Argonaut II* and—to the delight of the crowd—swept past the *Vizir* in a rare straight-line passing move.

He shot through the next archway—now in 8th position—and flying on adrenalin.

Moments later, he beheld the flashing yellow hover lights indicating the entrance to the Fiumicino Pits.

He banked left, aiming for the pits, thrilled to be where he was . . .

. . . when disaster struck.

Etienne Trouveau, it seemed, hadn't appreciated Jason's cheeky passing maneuver.

As Jason had banked to enter the pits, the Frenchman had accelerated unexpectedly and, in a shockingly rude maneuver, cut across Jason's nose—swiping it with his bladed Renault nosewing, slicing the right-hand wing of Jason's own nosewing clean off!

Jason watched in apoplectic horror as a piece of his car's nose fell away and tumbled into the sea like a skimming stone: a few bounces and a splash. At the same time, out of the corner of his eye, he saw Trouveau disappear into the pits to the left—

Swiping it with his bladed Renault nosewing

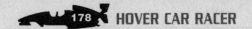

Then reality struck.

Hard.

510 mph is not a speed at which you want to lose control.

The *Argonaut II* lost control. First it lurched left—then it pitched dramatically to the right—touching the demag ripple strips, causing the car's magnetic power levels to plummet—before Jason engaged his compressed-air thrusters to get them off the debilitating strips.

The *Argonaut II* shot clear off the track, out to the right, *out over* the ripple strips—missing the entry to the pits completely—setting off in a *wide* arc out over the ocean, its mag levels plummeting even further down into the red.

It banked away to the right, out over the sea, out toward the far western horizon, and Jason realized to his horror that after the collision, *he could only steer to the right*.

Then things got worse.

His car slowed. Dramatically.

Thanks to the ripple strip, its magneto drives were now almost dry. The *Argonaut II*—with a broken nosewing and almost zero power—was limping out over the open sea, only capable of turning right.

"*Jason!*" Sally's voice called in his ear. "*You okay?*"

"We're okay . . ." Jason said through clenched teeth. "Just pissed. And I can only turn right."

"*What the heck was that? Is every French driver in this industry a jerk?*"

"Just stand by, Sally. We're not out of this yet. We're gonna try and make it to the pits . . ."

"How?"

"If we can only turn right, then we'll do it by only turning right . . ."

The *Argonaut II* puttered around in a painfully slow, painfully wide circle, a circuit easily several miles in circumference. But a circle that would end at—

—the pit entry.

"*But you're going to have to come back over the demag strip,*" Sally said.

"Then I hope we have enough power to take the hit," Jason said.

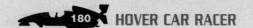

The *Argonaut II* limped around in its arc, at a pathetic 10 mph—it was almost unnatural to see a hover car moving at such a slow pace.

"Bug," Jason called, "do some calculations. How long is this circle going to take us?"

The Bug did the math in his head in about three seconds. He told Jason the answer.

"Three minutes!" Jason exclaimed. "*Minutes!* Dang . . ." As Jason well knew, hover car races were won by seconds, not minutes. Once you went down by more than a minute, your race was run.

But still he flew on.

As he did so, the Bug kept an eye on the pits, on the other cars in the field that were whizzing into them at full speed.

The Bug counted them off: 15th . . . 20th . . . 25th . . . 26th.

He informed Jason.

The 26th car had entered the pits.

They were now officially coming in last.

● ● ●

Three minutes later they came full circle, and Jason lined them up with the entrance to the Fiumicino Pits.

At this point, every other car in the race had sped off into the distance at full speed, leaving Jason alone, foundering off the coast.

But his situation had provided the crowd camped on the rocky coastline with a special spectacle—they were enjoying watching him struggle and as such, were cheering him on, shouting chants, clapping in unison, willing the *Argonaut II* into the pits.

Jason eyed the demag lights directly ahead of him, blocking his way to the pits. The last hurdle.

He checked his mag level display:

MAG 1	2.2%	2.3%	MAG 2
MAG 3	4.1%	2.4%	MAG 4
MAG 5	2.2%	2.3%	MAG 6

Five of his six mags were on 2 percent power, one a little over 4 percent.

As he'd learned back at Race School, in Race 25, a standard run over a demag ripple strip robbed you of 3 percent of magnetic power.

"I only need one percent to make it," he said grimly.

But as he also knew, if the *Argonaut II* lingered for too long over the ripple strip, it would lose more magnetic power than that—*all* his power—and that meant dropping out of the sky and into the water . . .

"Hang on, Bug. Here we go."

The *Argonaut II* banked round toward the pit entrance at 10 mph, heading right for the line of red demag lights.

The crowd hushed.

Jason held his breath.

The *Argonaut II* crossed the demag strip.

Jason's instrument panel squealed in panic, and his mag levels instantly changed:

MAG 1	0.0%	0.0%	MAG 2
MAG 3	1.1%	0.0%	MAG 4
MAG 5	0.0%	0.0%	MAG 6

The display started flashing and blinking like a Christmas tree. Red warning lights blazed everywhere.

The *Argonaut II* cleared the ripple strip—and by the time it did so, five of its mags were dead.

But one remained.

With a bare 1.1 percent power left on it, bearing Jason's entire car all on its own.

The *Argonaut II* was still moving—by the skin of its teeth.

The crowd on the coastline roared with delight.

And so, creeping, crawling, hobbling like a wounded soldier leaving the field of battle, the *Argonaut II* entered the pits—

Clank!—Clunk!—Hiss-wapp!

The Lombardi Team Tarantula worked fast.

Old mags came off. New mags went on. Compressed air hoses attached. A brand-new nosewing was attached. Coolant fluid went in.

Every indicator on Jason's dash display sprang to life— refreshed, renewed, recharged.

Jason looked around the pit area.

It was largely empty—all the other pit crews had left, heading for the second set of pits in Pescara on the other side of the country.

Jason searched the area, half hoping to see Scott

Syracuse somewhere nearby, but it was to no avail. Syracuse hadn't come.

Then the Tarantula lifted clear of the *Argonaut II* and Sally smacked the back of Jason's helmet: "Time to get back in this race! Go! Go! Go!"

Jason gunned everything he had and the *Argonaut II* blasted out of the pits, four whole minutes behind the pack, and headed back into the race.

Behind him, Sally immediately started loading up her stuff—she had to get to Pescara.

The main pack of racers rocketed down the toe of the boot that is Italy before shooting through the Straits of Messina and thus commencing the figure-8 round the islands of Sicily and Sardinia.

The crowds gathered on the coastlines of both islands cheered loudly as the jet fighter–like cars shot past them at a cool 500 mph.

But the loudest cheer of all came for the lonely last-placed car: the no. 2 car for the Lombardi Team, driven by the kid

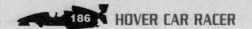

from the Race School, shooting along at full speed even though it was a hopeless four minutes behind the others.

The crowds loved it.

This lone Ferrari F-3000 couldn't possibly win the race *and yet it was still trying*.

Thanks to countless headset cell phones, word traveled along the coastline ahead of the *Argonaut II*, so that when it arrived at a new spot, a supergigantic Mexican Wave followed alongside it, the crowds urging it on.

The Lombardi Team hover trailer carrying Sally McDuff across Italy shoomed down the freeway in a lane specifically reserved for race crews heading for the pit area in Pescara.

Neither Sally nor her driver saw the two black Ford hover cars cruising down the highway behind them, keeping pace with their trailer . . .

. . . watching them.

When the main pack shot through the Straits of Messina for the second time and rounded the toe of Italy,

Alessandro Romba was in the lead, closely followed by Fabian and the second USAF car, with Xavier Xonora now having (impressively) moved up into 4th place.

Jason had closed to within two-and-a-half minutes of the main pack, but with the race now three-quarters over, barring a miracle, he was just making up the numbers.

Then the main pack bent right, shooting down the heel of Italy's boot—none of them taking the bait and entering the famously difficult shortcut.

Two-and-a-half minutes later, as the rest of them were rounding the base of the heel, Jason sighted Taranto, the town at the mouth of the shortcut.

The Bug said something.

"As a matter of fact," Jason replied, "I *am* thinking about taking the shortcut. Why? Why not? We're screwed as we are. Besides, you never know. We could get lucky."

The Bug offered some more advice.

"Ouch, man," Jason said. "Don't hold back or anything."

But the Bug wasn't finished.

"I know what Syracuse said," Jason retorted. "But he isn't here now, is he?"

"*I wouldn't say that . . .*" a voice said suddenly in Jason's earpiece.

It was the voice of Scott Syracuse.

Scott Syracuse sat in the back of the moving Lombardi Team trailer, alongside Sally McDuff, as it sped across Italy.

He had arrived in Rome only twenty minutes earlier, and had forced his way through the crowds, trying to get to the Fiumicino Pit Lane to meet Sally. But she'd left by the time he'd got there, so he'd chased her trailer down the highway in his black Ford and waved her down from the window of his speeding car.

As soon as he was on board the trailer, Sally had put him in radio contact with Jason.

"*Mr. Syracuse!*" Jason's voice came in over the speakers. "*You came!*"

"I'm sorry I couldn't be here earlier, Jason," Syracuse said, "but there have been some problems at the Race

School in your absence and I couldn't get away. But now that I'm here, I'm going to get you back in this race."

"*How?*"

Syracuse focused his eyes on the horizon. "When you hit Taranto, Jason, take the shortcut. If I can, I'm going to guide you through it."

As if the Italian crowds needed anything more to cheer about, they positively exploded when they saw the *Argonaut II* abruptly veer left and shoot toward the yawning Tunnel of Taranto, the wide concrete entry to the shortcut.

The *Argonaut II*—last and alone and absolutely delighting the masses—blasted into the tunnel.

A misty concrete-walled labyrinth, illuminated only by the *Argonaut II*'s winglights.

Jason slowed, surveying the tunnel system. The first junction he came to contained *six* forks.

Syracuse's voice said calmly: *"First junction, take the ten o'clock fork."*

Jason did it, banking left, heading down into the Earth.

The next junction also had six forks. And the next and the next.

But Syracuse's directions were precise. *"Take the two o'clock fork—straight ahead—ninety degree right-hand turn—"*

Down they went, deeper into the tunnel system, before suddenly the tunnel junctions became even more complex: now they contained *eight* forks—with two extra tunnels shooting vertically upward and downward from the center of each new fork.

"*Vertically down*," Syracuse said when they came to the first eight-pronged junction.

"Down?" Jason queried. "We're gonna hit the Earth's core soon."

"*Yes. Down*," Syracuse said firmly.

But then he directed them sideways once again and after a few more junctions their tunnels started to take an upwardly-sloping trajectory.

"*Now take the ten o'clock fork at the next junction*," Syracuse said, "*And get ready . . .*"

"Get ready?" Jason asked. "For what—"

He took the next fork as directed and—*bam*—his eyes were assaulted by blinding sunlight and the sight of the glittering Adriatic Sea, the blue cloudless sky, the seaside mansions of the city of Bari, and the rugged eastern

Down they went, deeper into the tunnel system.

coast of Italy stretching away from him to the north.

As the *Argonaut II* exploded out from the cliffside exit tunnel to the shortcut, pandemonium broke out among the spectators gathered on the headland all around it. Their collective roar of joy could be heard twenty miles away.

The Bug squealed with delight.

Jason swallowed in disbelief.

They'd made it!

They'd come out the other side of the shortcut!

But before Jason could revel too much in his achievement—*shoom!-shoom!-shoom!*—he was overshot by three hover cars. The cars of:

Alessandro Romba.

Fabian.

And Angus Carver of the USAF Racing Team.

The fourth car to bank around him was Xavier Xonora's Lockheed, and in a fleeting instant, Jason glimpsed the Black Prince's sideways-turned face and his look of pure shock. Xavier obviously hadn't expected to see Jason again in this race.

Even more satisfying was the car Jason saw in his side mirrors—the purple and gold Renault of Etienne Trouveau, the nasty French racer who had almost put Jason out of the race. The *Argonaut II* had come out of the shortcut *ahead* of Trouveau!

It took Jason a second to absorb it all.

He and the Bug had just made up three whole minutes on the rest of the field, and in doing so had gone from last to 5th.

"Thanks, Mr. Syracuse!" he said into his radio. "You just got us back in this race!"

As Sally's team trailer entered the outskirts of Pescara, every single giant-screen television in the town was showing replays of the *Argonaut II* blasting out from the short cut.

Every commentator on every TV and radio station was astonished at the *Argonaut*'s recovery. Last to 5th in one fell swoop. *Fifth!* They couldn't believe it. And with the second series of pit stops due in Pescara in about ten minutes, the race was now officially on.

But with that news, as if on cue, the second black Ford that had been following Sally's trailer across the country suddenly accelerated, pulling ahead of the Lombardi trailer.

And as the two vehicles zoomed underneath a freeway overpass, the black Ford suddenly jackknifed sideways, inexplicably cutting across the front of the Team Lombardi trailer, smashing into its front bumper, forcing it off the road and directly into a concrete pylon supporting the overpass.

With a terrible crunching sound, the Lombardi trailer smashed into the pylon, and crumpled like a giant concertina—while the black Ford simply drove off, darting into the distance, disappearing.

Everyone inside the trailer was thrown forward by the impact—the driver, Sally, Syracuse—but luckily they were all wearing seat belts and the trailer was equipped with compressed-air safety blasters that acted like the airbags of old.

The exterior of the trailer, however, was completely ruined.

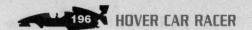

And as Sally unbuckled herself from her seat, she realized the situation: She was only two minutes' drive away from the pits. But on foot, that would take . . .

. . . about ten minutes.

Syracuse knew the score as well.

"Grab a hand truck and load it up with mags," he said. "And start running."

Ten minutes later, the leaders entered the Pescara pits. The hover cars roared into the pits in single file before branching off into their allotted pit bays.

Their pit crews were waiting.

Alessandro Romba led the way, followed by Fabian. Then the USAF pilot, Carver, Xavier Xonora, and . . . Jason Chaser.

The *Argonaut II* swung into its pit bay . . .

. . . to find no one there.

"Sally!" Jason yelled into his radio. "Where are you!"

A second later, Jason saw Trouveau slide into his pit bay across the way. Trouveau glared at Jason as his pit machine went to work on his car. But when Trouveau realized that Jason had no pit crew around him, his fierce glare became an evil smile.

At that moment, Pablo Riviera's Ferrari shoomed into the adjoining Lombardi pit bay and his crew went to work. If they could have, they would have helped Jason, but they *were* Riviera's crew, so they had to service his car first.

"Where the heck is Sally!" Jason yelled. Every second he lost here felt like an hour—

"I'm coming!" Sally yelled, appearing from a nearby doorway at a run, pushing a hover hand truck stacked with magneto drives and some coolant bottles. Her face and hair were drenched with sweat—she'd been running for some time. Behind her, also pushing a hover hand truck, was Scott Syracuse.

Shoom. Romba shot out of the pits.

Sally and Syracuse came alongside the *Argonaut II*. Sally immediately started unloading magneto drives from her hand truck, while Syracuse simply hit a button on his truck— causing the entire thing to mechanically unfold *and rise*, transforming itself into: a portable Tarantula pit machine. Sally clipped new mags to the Tarantula's waiting arms, while its other arms started demagging the *Argonaut II*.

Shoom. Fabian shot out of the pits.

To save time, Sally poured coolant fluid into the *Argonaut II*'s tanks by hand. Emptied one bottle. Chucked it. Emptied another. Chucked that one, too.

"Come *on*!" Jason urged.

God, he thought, *after all we've been through in this race, how can this be happening!*

Shoom. Shoom. Shoom.

Carver, Xavier, and Trouveau all left the pits.

The Tarantula rose up and spread its arms wide—finished.

"Sally . . . !"

"Just . . . one . . . more . . . second . . ." Sally grimaced as she jammed some fresh compressed-air cylinders into the *Argonaut II*'s rear-thruster nozzles.

Shoom. Riviera exited the pits.

Then Sally yanked her hands away.

"Clear!" she yelled. "*Go! Go! Go!*"

Jason punched it and the *Argonaut II* roared out of the pits—in 7th place—and entered the final stages of the Italian Run.

THE ITALIAN RUN:
ROME TO VENICE II
Venice II Gauntlet

═══ **Course**

▭ **Bridge**

ITALY

Venice II

Sardinia

Rome

Sicily

The stage was set for a killer finish.

The setting was spectacular: where the seas on the other side of Italy were dark and rough, here the Adriatic shone like a flat turquoise jewel.

And the finishing stages of the Italian Run were notoriously difficult: This would be no full-speed dash to the Finish Line. After they raced up the coast, the racers would face two fiendishly curved sections of track: the tight and twisting—and identical—Grand Canals of Venice and Venice II. The second of these two sections was so intense it had a name: the Venice II Gauntlet.

• • •

The field thundered up the coast, bending and banking, swooping left and right to take the archways, kicking up spectacular geyser trails behind them.

Romba was out in front, tussling with Fabian for the lead.

Then there was a gap before the next bunch of racers: Carver, Xavier, Trouveau, and Riviera—with Jason hard on their heels.

Behind him, there was another cluster, led by Kamikaze Ideki in his Yamaha.

Venice came into view. Not Venice II, but the original waterborne city.

The racers shot up and around the fish-shaped island before swinging back south—and rocketing into the Grand Canal from the north. The Grand Canal takes the shape of a wide, swooping reverse S and is flanked on either side by high and historic buildings.

Into the city they went, low and fast, spraying geyser trails as they shot underneath the first of the three bridges that span the Grand Canal, the Ponte dei Scalzi.

Indeed, it was a geyser trail that allowed Jason to get up

into 6th place—Etienne Trouveau had seen Pablo Riviera trying to overtake him, so Trouveau had lowered the *Vizir* slightly at the Ponte dei Scalzi and cut across Riviera's path, causing his geyser trail to spray all over Riviera's cockpit.

Blinded by the sudden spray, Riviera had flailed away to the left, out of control, under the bridge, and rocketed like a missile *straight at* an eighteenth-century church—

—where his Ferrari lurched to a sudden, springing halt, caught in the hover car equivalent of a gravel trap: a magnetic Dead Zone. Naturally, all of Venice's buildings were protected by these negatively charged dead zones—so that no piece of history could be destroyed by a crashing hover car.

And suddenly Jason—skimming along behind the two racers—was in 6th place and right on the hammer of Etienne Trouveau.

Both cars banked hard, almost at 90 degrees, as they navigated the swinging bends of the Grand Canal. Under the Rialto Bridge with its enclosed shops, then through

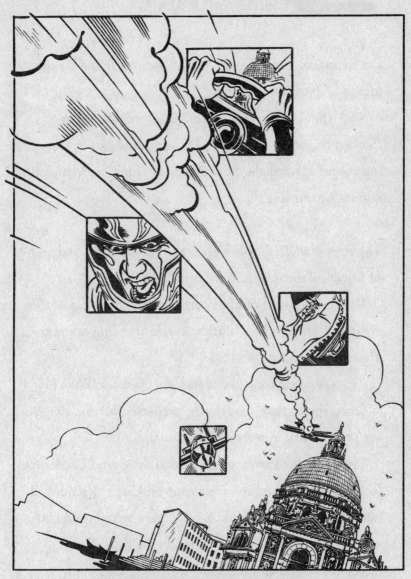

Straight at an eighteenth-century church

the wooden Accademia Bridge—Jason flying within inches of Trouveau's tailfin.

And then they were back out over the open sea, flanked by pleasure liners and hover grandstands, shooting round toward the final sector of the race: Venice II and its Grand Canal.

The *Argonaut II* shot low over the Adriatic, the Renault of Etienne Trouveau right in front of it.

Venice II loomed on the horizon, its high replica of the great Bell Tower of St. Mark's Square standing tall in the afternoon light.

"This is where we make our move," Jason told the Bug.

Once again, they shot north, preparing for the swinging reverse turn into the Grand Canal.

Jason saw the yawning entrance to the Grand Canal off to his right: flanked by apartment buildings that looked just like those of Old Venice, only these were brand new.

Trouveau hit the Grand Canal on the fly.

Jason charged in after him.

Blurred city buildings rushed by him on either side.

And then Trouveau tried to do to Jason what he had done to Riviera—at the New Ponte dei Scalzi, he cut right, raising a curtain of spraying water across the *Argonaut*'s path.

But Jason's reactions were up to the challenge—he stayed right, and rather than slowing down, he gunned his thrusters, rushing perilously close to the dead zone protecting the New Ponte dei Scalzi—and pressed between Trouveau's Renault and the bridge's swooping arch, he banked up on his side, going a full 90 degrees, and with barely an inch on either side . . .

. . . he rocketed out from under the bridge and shot past Trouveau's Renault—now in 5th place!

Trouveau swore. But not before Kamiko Ideki tried to seize the opportunity and swoop past him as well. But Trouveau wasn't going to allow that and he banged against the side of the Kamikaze's Yamaha, fighting him to the finish.

As for Jason, the black V-shaped tailfin of Xavier Xonora's 4th-placed Lockheed-Martin now loomed before him, banking right, taking the sweeping right-hander that led under the Rialto Bridge.

Jason did the math quickly: With only two turns to go, there just wasn't enough racetrack left to catch Xavier before the Finish Line.

Which meant, if he kept his head, he could finish 5th in his first Grand Slam race—not a bad effort at all. Just finishing was an achievement, but 5th was simply awesome. And beating that creep Trouveau would be even more satisfying. . . .

Under the Rialto. The crowds roaring. Venice II rushing by him on either side.

Then banking left. The crowds going nuts. Shooting under the Accademia Bridge, after which Jason straightened and suddenly, gloriously . . .

. . . the end of the Grand Canal came into view, the point where it opened out into a wide harborlike bay, flanked by the redbrick Bell Tower of St. Mark's Square on the left and the giant dome of the Basilica di Santa Maria della Salute on the right. Only today, beyond the two colossal structures stood a massive alloy arch, hovering above the water of the bay, covered in checkered flags and a huge digital scoreboard . . .

The Finish Line.

Jason's eyes lit up.

The end was in sight. They'd done it.

It would be the last time he'd smile in a very long time.

For it was at that precise moment that a small explosive device attached to the tailfin of the *Argonaut II* went off.

It was about the size of a pinhead, hardly even noticeable to the naked eye.

An ultraconcentrated military explosive made of SDX-III epoxy. It was used by commando teams to blow open doors. A fraction of an ounce was enough to destroy the average reinforced door—more than enough to completely destroy the lightweight polycarbonate tailfin of a hover car.

It had been surreptitiously placed on the tail of the *Argonaut II* by a light-fingered hand in the last few moments before the Italian Run had begun.

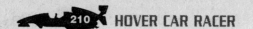

• • •

The tailfin of the *Argonaut II* blasted outward in a shower of tiny pieces.

Jason immediately lost all control. At 460 mph—his Ferrari lurching downward with shocking suddenness. He grappled with the steering wheel, but it did absolutely nothing in response.

He looked up and saw the Finish Line approaching and for a brief instant, thought they might make it over the line—

—but then the whole horizon rolled dramatically and suddenly they were traveling on their side, almost upside down—which meant ejecting was not possible—so that now all Jason saw was the surface of the Grand Canal rushing up toward his eyes.

"Bug! Hold on! This is going to be really bad!"

It was bad.

The *Argonaut II* slammed into the surface of the Grand Canal with a terrible splash.

It hit the water nosefirst, then tumbled three times, sending debris shooting out in every direction, before—*whack!*—it smacked down on the surface of the Canal and lurched to a halt, floating *upside down*: its underside pointing skyward, its cockpit underwater.

Every single person in Italy, whether at the track or watching at home, stood up and gasped.

The silent underwater world.

Holding his breath, Jason quickly unclasped his seat belt. He spun, suspended in the water, and saw the Bug grappling with his own seat belt.

Jason could see that the Bug needed help, but before he could help him, Jason needed more air himself.

He swam four feet upward and broke the surface—to see the high buildings of Venice II flanking the canal all around him; to hear the crowd cheer briefly, glad to see him alive.

He was taking a deep breath when he saw them.

Saw Etienne Trouveau and Kamiko Ideki round the

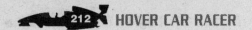

final turn together, emerging from under the Accademia Bridge, banging into each other, fighting to the end.

And in that instant, it happened.

Trouveau got ahead of Ideki and performed his signature move—he cut across Ideki's nosewing and sheared it off with his own bladed nosewing.

The Japanese racer's nosewing fell clear off, splashing down into the canal, and Ideki—in a panic, desperate to finish the race—tried to avoid the safe landing that the nearest dead zone alongside the Grand Canal would have provided him.

Instead, he grappled with his steering wheel and pulled his Yamaha up—but he hadn't counted on how quickly he would lose altitude.

And he realized the truth of his situation too late.

His Yamaha was going to smash directly into the *Argonaut II*, helpless on the surface of the Grand Canal.

Ideki may have realized it too late, but Jason, still treading water, saw exactly what was going to happen.

Jason saw exactly what was going to happen.

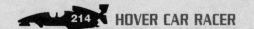

The Kamikaze's Yamaha was going to slam into the *Argonaut II* . . . and the Bug was still trapped in it under the surface!

Jason gauged the distance and the Kamikaze's screaming speed: impact would come in about five seconds.

And so, with the out-of-control Yamaha zooming like a guided missile toward his upside-down hover car, Jason took a deep breath and went under to try and free the Bug in time.

Underwater again.

Frantically swimming in his flight suit, Jason came to the Bug, and saw that his brother's seat belt buckle had jammed. It wasn't coming free.

The Bug was in a fearful panic—tearing at his buckle, screaming underwater, yelling bubbles.

And in that instant, Jason saw the future.

This would take more than five seconds.

Kamiko Ideki's Yamaha shot through the air like a bullet.

A moment before it hit the *Argonaut II*, two blurring

objects could be seen rocketing up into the sky above it—the ejection seats of Ideki and his navigator.

Then without slowing or stopping or even veering to the side, the Yamaha slammed into the stationary *Argonaut* at a shocking 435 mph.

The impact of hover car on hover car shook the world.

And the ensuing flaming explosion filled the Grand Canal, expanding across its breadth in a billowing orange cloud.

Pieces of the *Argonaut II* rained down on the canal for a full minute, creating a thousand tiny splashes.

A deathly hush descended upon the crowds gathered in the grandstands around the Finish Line. Sitting in his own VIP box, Umberto Lombardi could only stare at the horrific scene in disbelief.

The *Argonaut* was gone—blasted to nothing.

And with it: Jason Chaser and the Bug.

"Oh . . . my . . . Lord . . ." Lombardi breathed.